CW01432256

# The Incredible Mr. Black

**Blackstone, Book 1, Volume 1**

Rachel E. Rice

Published by Rachel E. Rice, 2024.

**Mr. Blackstone**
**The Incredible Mr. Black**
**By Rachel E Rice**

# Table of Contents

Author's Note: This Book has been re-edited for your reading enjoyment.

The first three books should be read in order. In Book 1 the title has been changed to Mr. Blackstone. There are now nine books in this suspense, erotic romance thriller. Book 10 coming in 2023 and book 11 Black Ice in 2024

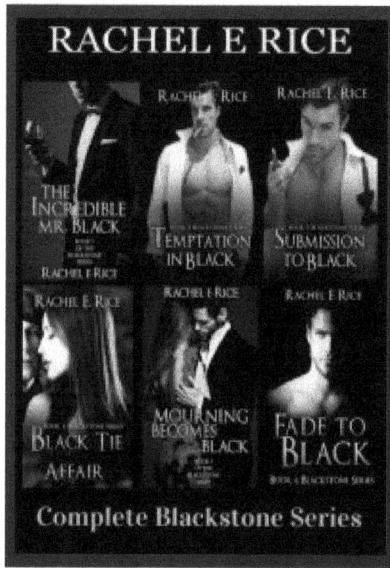

AUTHOR'S NOTE: THIS book has been re-edited for your reading pleasure. Enjoy!

You can purchase these books everywhere.

Sign up at my blog Rachel E Rice[1] for chapter reveals, free books, and the latest books before they are published. You can contact me at: rachelerice04@gmail.com Thank you for reading my books. Please leave a review. Enjoy! Blog Rachel E Rice[2]

1.    https://rachel-e-rice.com/books/
2.    https://rachel-e-rice.com/books/

When Maximilian Blackstone, who is into bondage and S&M, meets a young woman named Alexander, he instantly falls in love with her. However, on the first night she sleeps with him, and then she discovers his secrets, which includes a twin brother who is more damaged than him. Alex, as Max calls her, has a few secrets of her own.

Alex matches wits with Max to change him, but she soon falls under his spell, and is willing to do anything for him except for one thing. Is she willing to step into his world of bondage and S&M without losing herself?

This book contains a secret baby, bondage, ropes, and plenty of secrets.

## Mr. Blackstone

# Chapter 1

The worst thing a young woman could do was fall in love, and worse yet was to fall in love with a sexy, handsome, drop-dead gorgeous rich man. Because you could find yourself doing things you never would imagine—like letting him handcuff you to his bed, as he made passionate, sexual, erotic love to you.

Driving into the gated community, shivering from the thought, I stopped to put in the code. The mansion was sitting on a lush green manicured grassy hill with a circular driveway. I brought my SL500 Mercedes to a quick stop and exited it, another present I'd accepted from the billionaire industrialist, Maximilian Blackstone, or as I called him, Mr. Black.

A young man reached for my keys. I stiffened my hand. He felt my hand hesitate. "Don't worry, miss, we'll take care of your car." It wasn't the car that worried me.

Walking in a daze, I was now at the front door of Pandora's Retreat, a luxurious getaway for the serious bondage and S&M enthusiast. My mind wavered as I count my steps. I couldn't decide whether I wanted to do this, whether I wanted to walk through those double glass doors with the gold-plated trim, and spend a week experiencing a world of BDSM.

I'd had only one man in my sexual life, and I couldn't imagine anyone who could match the Incredible Mr. Black, Max as his friends called him.

I tugged the collar of my cream-colored silk shirt and lumbered on through the doors. My gaze turned, following an attractive woman heading in my direction, where a faint light bounced off her stern face. She stopped to greet me, "Welcome, Ms. Johns. You will find your stay most delightful, and you will discover that we have attended to all your needs, including an apartment for a week's stay." The director, a beautiful golden-haired woman of forty, wearing a black fitted dress and high heels, who appeared to enjoy her job, smiled warmly, opening the door of the apartment, and handed me the key.

*How did it come to this? Why did I agree to do this?* I wondered, ignoring the answer.

Three years ago, I fell in love, and the last thing I thought about was being a sex slave to a beautiful exotic-looking billionaire who appeared on the outside normal, but by my standards then, there was nothing normal about whippings, ropes, and handcuffs. I guessed a few years ago, I would have been considered vanilla.

I was here to meet the Master, he was to teach me how to be the perfect sub and bring me to a higher level of submission. Mr. Black suggested that I was confused, and I didn't know whether I was a sub or Dom, and he needed a sub. I knew what I was, he just couldn't handle it. Finally, I agreed to his wishes, but I warned him that sending me here could be dangerous for both of us. But deep down inside, I was anxious to learn about the real world of bondage, because until now, I had been faking it to understand, and fit into the world of my incredible handsome and sexy, Mr. Black.

*When did this begin?* I asked myself as I prepared my mind and body for what I had come to love. When did I begin to enjoy a man placing me over his knee, whipping my ass, and tying me to his headboard, while fucking me senseless?

It started the day I answered an ad in the local newspaper for a terrific job in Montana, never bothering to read the small print.

Today was my first day on the job. I was suffering from jet lag, incompetence, identity crisis, and a host of other insecurities that a twenty-two-year-old who had just completed college, with mountains of debt, no friends or family to speak of, and a new job that I needed. I'd found this position in the New York Post: *Wanted, young gregarious go getter to work in sales. She should be intelligent, a college graduate, pretty without being noticeable, comfortable with individuals who are among the one percent...* The ad went on and on. I figured I had one of the qualities they advertised, and I packed my bags and headed to Billings, Montana in the middle of ski season.

I wasn't a drop-dead gorgeous woman, but I had my moments, just average, long auburn curly hair worn in a ponytail most often, oval face, high cheekbones, and large blue eyes. I never trusted my looks as a magnet for men.

I never got the impression that the company which hired me was more interested in my looks than whether I could do the job.

"Miss Bishop," the manager, Joshua said, holding my resumé and looking over his glasses, "Can you work overtime?" That was it. Staring at him as his eyes glanced intermittently at me; I thought he was a great-looking guy, with dirty-blond hair, barely six feet, and a great body—the kind of body you would get from farm work, not spending time in a gym.

They must have been desperate for personnel, but you couldn't tell by the beautiful scenery, luxurious accommodations for the staff and guests, all the food you could eat, and the pay was great. I would have paid them to work at Blackstone Ski Lodge.

I soon learned that the altitude was unbearable, and on one occasion I almost fainted. My skin stayed dry, and I had to keep a supply of Vaseline and ChapStick in my imitation leather purse. I was constantly licking my lips and batting my eyes, because I wasn't used to makeup. One of the hotel guests, an older gentleman, thought I was flirting with him. He was all of seventy.

"Get a life," I said.

Shuffling off none too happy, he tried to have me fired, but Joshua intervened, and that was why he and I became best buds, besides he let me sleep on his couch, because I was afraid to live alone. I was sure he expected much more, but that was all I had to give. I planned on remaining a virgin until the right man came along, handsome and rich, but that was just a dream, the problem was it was as easy to fall in love with a rich man as a poor one, but probabilities were that I would never meet a rich handsome man that would even take a look at me, and say, "She's the one."

It was the middle of the winter ski season, and the hotel was shorthanded. Jacob took his time getting to the counter, because he liked his long lunches with the newly hired. He claimed he wanted to do a detailed interview. I knew better, but I owed him just for taking a chance on me.

Reaching for my ChapStick under the counter, I stooped, and when I raised my head, I gazed directly into the eyes of the most gorgeous man I had ever seen. Living in New York, I had seen my share of men. I had seen all races, all nationalities, all ages, gay and straight, and he was just beautiful—a face like none I had ever seen. His wide dark green eyes, a strong jaw, head full of dark curls cut short, thick eyebrows, and he wore a hidden smile, or was that a smirk, the kind I had seen on a billboard for a Tom Ford advertisement for Tom Ford Noir, a fragrance for men.

Yes, Noir, it meant Black, how fitting.

He was just different. I felt it throughout my body. My legs tingled, my hands shook, and my mouth opened wide. He was the one, the one I would do anything for, the one I would give up my virginity for in a fast second, if only he would ask with just a whisper in my ear.

This did not say much about my self-control. I thought I had plenty until I laid eyes on him. "Wow!" His breathtaking sinful face should have been concealed, to prevent him from casting a spell on all women who gazed into his green eyes. Those eyes appeared capable of seeing through a woman's dress and straight to her clit.

Gliding into the lodge, he was chatting and laughing, but paused when our eyes locked. Stopping in his tracks, there was a moment of silence, and then his gaze wandered around the room, and the room filled again with idle chatter.

I knew he was trouble when I scanned his gorgeous face and body. He strutted through a throng of eligible beautiful obscene young men and women with all eyes targeting him. They leaned and whispered, obviously they knew him. Dressed immaculately in a black Giorgio Armani suit, black and white Prada shirt, and black Gucci loafers, walking with a sort of swagger, leaning as he walked—like a predatory cat, lumbering through the double doors of the Blackstone Ski Lodge in Billings, Montana, with an entourage of three handsome men trailing behind his gorgeous firm muscular ass. His jet-black curly hair was tousled, and windswept, his piercing green eyes begging me to lie down and stay awhile to be his sex slave on call, I thought, remembering that moment. I kept playing it over in my mind. *Wow.*

This man was trouble for any woman crazy enough to fall in love with him. So, I convinced myself, *Keep your wits about you, and don't act like a frigging idiot. It's far too late for that,* I admitted.

Joshua returned just in time. "Sorry, Alex, I owe you one."

"Oh, that's okay," I said, following that handsome fuck's gaze. I heard nothing and saw nothing. I was staring into space, dreaming, and heading in the direction of the elevators, trying to get out of the room before I fainted.

I stepped aside, to allow the entourage and that man I would die for into the elevator, hesitating, praying the door would close. Too late, he turned around, his face expressive and light with a skillful grin, a disarming smile he used to great effect. Facing the open door and space that I now occupied, he said, "That's a lovely necklace." His voice, deep with perfect English, of prep-schools and elite colleges and universities, seduced me, surprised me, and then the elevator, closed immediately... in my goofy-looking face.

My head gave a quick jerk downward to see what he was looking at. I grabbed for my turquoise drop held by a black string, the only piece

"Yes? Hello," I responded, like the idiot I claimed I would never become if I laid eyes on him again.

"Ms. Bishop... I was wondering if... I want... I would like to see you," he said with a sexy English tone to his voice.

"Why?" I leaned forward. "Did you say you want to see me, sir, ah Mr. Black... I mean Mr. Blackstone," I sounded incompetent, like I had escaped from an asylum.

"Forget it. I'm sorry," he said, fading away into the private elevator. I stood staring at the spot where he had asked to see me with my mouth so wide it could have caught a fly, if any could survive at this altitude. A man like that asking to see me, did he mean what I thought he meant? Me? Alexander Bishop, a girl who had never been anywhere except Brooklyn, well, I could count the states, breathing the same air as this rich, handsome, drop-dead gorgeous fuck. He looked all of thirty-five, so I rationalized that he was too old, too worldly, and too dangerous for me.

And what did he mean by "wanting to see me?" Was I reading too much in those few words? Joshua said I would analyze things to death, but I couldn't understand why a man who was obviously articulate, would just say, "I want to see you."

If I was stupid enough to dream that he thought I was attractive, or entertain such an idea, all I could do was get hurt. I had no defense. I wasn't worldly, I had one friend, I had no money, and I wasn't that pretty.

What kind of experience did I have to even talk to that world-class man? Maybe he was married, and I would be one of the many girls he fucked on vacation, but for me it would be a fuck of a lifetime. I might never recover if he put his rich dick inside me. *I would be gone, probably turn into a stalker,* I thought. So, it was better that I get him out of my mind, but I couldn't. He haunted my thoughts, my body, and my clit.

A chill eased up my back, caressing my spine, straight into the nape of my neck, and settling on the roots of my hair. *Wow!* It was then I knew that I would do anything for him, and that was dangerous.

The next day I figured the best way to rid myself of Mr. Black was to try out my new skis, maybe break a leg or something, and have them send me back to Brooklyn with workman's comp. That would help me until I could get another job and get far away from him.

I had lied on my application, and stated that I was proficient on the slopes, so they gave me skis, and lessons were free to upgrade my skills. What skills? Bending forward adjusting the skis, I stepped backwards and backed up until I hit a wall, or so I thought. Looking through my legs, I saw a pair of skis with two long legs covered in a black ski suit standing behind me. It was Mr. Black's rock-hard body. There he stood all six foot two, in a black ski suit and gear, and my ass plastered directly on his hard dick.

He didn't move. His gaze scanned my hair, back, and my ass. By the look in his eyes, he appeared to be measuring the split of my butt for something, and I didn't know what? I couldn't straighten up, my finger had gotten stuck, and when I unhinged it and stood, he never moved. He stood on my skis with a wicked smile, and with me not moving an inch, I said wryly, "I hope you're enjoying yourself. Take a picture it'll last longer." That was all I could think of.

"Well, Ms. Bishop," he said with a sly smile crossing his inviting lips, "We meet again." I stood up with his body close, where not even a sheet of paper could pass between us, as if we were entwined in intercourse and he had penetrated my ass. He whispered softly in my ear, my butt quivering against his dick, with him getting even closer, if that was possible. He circled my body with his arms, and said, "You smell wonderful."

"Thank you, but could you get off of my skis?"

He moved his hand caressing my chin, then placed it lower. "Your beautiful neck needs something, a collar," he stated casually, passing his fingers from front to the back causing me to shiver, not from the cold, but from the heat of his penis penetrating my clothing like lightning. At the time I thought nothing of his comments. Maybe that was what the rich would say when they wanted to make a pass, and I responded in a childish and girlish manner.

"You smell pretty good yourself," was all I could get out, and then I froze. I should have asked, *"What the fuck are you doing?"* But I didn't. I should have asked, *"Have you lost your fucking mind?"* But I didn't. I should have asked, *"Do you think I'm that kind of girl? Do you want to fuck me?"* But I didn't.

"I was wondering whether I can see you under different circumstances," he said, a hint of vulnerability dancing in his green eyes, which had softened.

I managed to slightly turn my head. "You are seeing me now, why do you wish to see me? And please, get off of my skis," I said coldly, trying to cool the heat that was coursing between my thighs.

When I finally moved my skis to turn to face my fears, the obstruction was gone and so was Mr. Blackstone. So, here I was again staring into nothingness with only a mountain of snow for company, and feeling stupid once more. I swore to myself that if I saw him again, I would give him a piece of my mind—how dared he quit so soon. One minute more and I would have caved in, and he could have fucked me in my ears if he had a mind to.

I headed down the slope and at the very foot; I tripped, stumbled, rolled, and landed in a large bed of snow with my skis buried. I tried to stand, but that was impossible. I knew that I had sprained my ankle. Looking around, I didn't see anyone. I panicked and screamed, "Hello! I need help, I'm hurt!" Before I could yell again, standing in front of me was the extraordinary handsome, Mr. Black.

He rushed over to me, dug me out with a small shovel he carried somewhere, unfastened my skis, and lifted me like a doll. Cradled in his arms, my breath ceased. Gazing into my eyes, he asked, "Are you hurt?"

"It's my ankle." He touched it gently. I screamed not from pain, but desperate wanting his attention.

"You can't take pain, pain can be exciting and satisfying," he said, flashing a smile. "You know, childbirth is painful and satisfying."

"What did you say?" I always missed his cues.

"I guess we can't have children," he said, passing a dark teasing smirk along his mouth while not taking his eyes off me. His gaze unnerved me. "I can carry you to my cabin it's nearby. You're so light." I felt incredibly light, or I was incredibly stupid. He could be some kind of serial killer, or worse, a man who would make love to me and never see me again. Nevertheless, I felt comfortable in his arms, like I belonged there.

Stopping at a large house built with logs, he lumbered up the stone stairs with me in his arms, to this unbelievable redwood cabin in the middle of snow and mountains. I had never seen a house of that magnitude. It was built on a mountain with boulders as steps. Strong floor-to-ceiling glass windows surrounded the house, giving a panoramic view of everything for miles. The cabin was breathtaking, and it matched the owner—rich, beautiful, strong, and different.

We entered the house, and I turned around mystified at the décor. The foyer wide like a museum had numerous gray leather chairs placed facing the windows, large paintings lined the walls. The house stood half on the mountain and half on large pillars the kind you would find under bridges. "This place is beautiful."

"You are beautiful," he said, making me uncomfortable. Turning around I spied a large roaring fire.

"Oh, I love a fire." He placed me in a large cream leather chair, sitting near the huge fireplace, then picked up a log and began feeding the fire. It must have been his favorite chair, because it sat alone with a large table near with books sitting on it, and a small crystal chest set. He watched deliberately as I acted like a little girl who had never had anything or been anywhere, and he was right.

Trying to stand, I wobbled, he rushed to me and knelt looking up at me. "You can't walk on that leg. I will have the doctor here to examine it." His voice was commanding and strong.

"What about my job?"

"Joshua can get someone to replace you until you are fit for work. Remember they work for me and so do you, so relax, and let me pamper you." My mind began to work overtime, trying to figure out what it was he was after, and why me? He stood, walked away, turned, and smiled, then strutted into an area that appeared to be a kitchen. He came back moments later with a bottle of wine, two glasses, and a tin of Beluga caviar.

Wrinkling my nose at the caviar, Max looked at me confused. "Is something wrong, Alex?" I loved the way the sound of my name dripped from his lips—so authoritative, so masculine. No man had ever called me Alex; they always wanted to feminize Alexander. My parents named me after Alexander the Great, the great conqueror.

"Drinking wine is not good for me, I have a low tolerance for wine, and the caviar is from a mammal, it's like eating my own eggs," I said, looking at him thinking I'd said something interesting. But the truth was I had never tasted caviar. I could tell by his smile and arched eyebrow that I wasn't fooling him.

"Oh, you are one of those," he said, staring as if he had seen an alien. "After today with your ankle, I thought you needed a drink. And the caviar, I'll get rid of it. I'll have my cook make you something more familiar." He scooped up the silver tray, holding the tin of caviar, with silver matching spoons, and disappeared into the kitchen, then he returned looking disappointed and vulnerable. "I instructed my chef to make you soup, a sandwich, and a salad, you do eat lettuce?"

"Mr. Blackstone, I'll have the wine..."

He interrupted, "Call me Maximilian or Max." He poured the wine, and I took a sip and before I could finish it someone rang the bell. It was the doctor. He examined me and my ankle, massaged it, gave me some muscle relaxants, and said that I should stay off it for twenty-four hours and I would be good to go. Max didn't leave me. He sat and waited for the doctor to finish examining me. The last thing I remembered was looking into Max's beautiful face.

Waking in the middle of the night to the moon flowing through the picture windows, I worried, because I had fallen asleep around a man I didn't know. Was it the wine, or did Mr. Black slip something into my drink? No, it was the meds. He didn't have to drug me; I would give myself freely and happily, and he knew it. I felt my clothing. I was wearing a silk white top and nothing else. I felt the bed, now I knew what silk black sheets felt like. I smiled. I guessed he liked black. In the moonlight I saw a tall figure standing with his legs crossed in the doorway, his hand on his hip. "Are you okay?"

"Who undressed me? How did you know my size?"

He answered one of my questions. "Me. We are adults after all," he said, inching in my direction.

"We may be adults, but you are my employer," I said, wincing. "I'll never be able to look at you without feeling uncomfortable."

"Well, you will not have to see me again unless you want to." He strutted close to the bed and sat at the corner staring down at me. "Do you find me attractive?"

"What kind of question is that?" *A blind woman would find him attractive just from his voice. Doesn't he know how handsome and sexy he is, especially in the moonlight?*

"I was taken with you the moment I saw your beautiful face," he said with a secret smile.

*You weren't looking at my face it was my breasts, you sexy fuck.* Was he serious? Maybe he was blind, and I hadn't noticed. Maybe he had a missing leg, or he was impotent, and he would seduce anyone he could fool? *Why me?*

All possibilities crossed my mind, I came to a conclusion—I didn't care. He leaned over to kiss me. I leaned back away from his full lips.

"I don't think we should do this." *I was going to, but I didn't want to go easy.*

"I won't tell if you don't," he said with a gleeful smile.

"I'm not what you think I am?" I said, trying for respectability.

"You are exactly what I think you are?" he said with a twist of his head.

"Some kind of slut you can give wine to, and I'll do anything to be near a rich good-looking guy like you?"

"So, you find me appealing."

"Well, yes, in a kind of sexy odd way."

"Now I'm sexy?" he questioned with a soft smile and glowing eyes. He moved closer and leaned in to me. I tried to move away when he draped his muscular arm across my lap and trapped me.

"I didn't quite mean it like that."

"What if I told you that I'm attracted to you?" Mr. Black said, eyes penetrating my glance.

"What if I told you that I'm not attracted to you," I said, wanting to take those words back the minute they slipped from my lips.

"Then, I'm hurt. Feel my heart, it's broken." Mr. Black took my hand and placed it to his hard chest. I felt his heart beating quickly as he nudged his face closer to my neck. My body responded to his closeness. His hand pushed my hair to the side, and he planted kisses on my neck, on my chin, and on my lips.

First, a soft kiss, then one on the nape of my neck. He placed his strong manicured hand around my back to brace me, threading his hand through my curly unruly auburn hair, and said, "I'm turned on by your lips, which makes me want to..." He didn't finish his thoughts. He strummed his finger over my top lip. *Maybe it was too soon for him to say that he wanted me to wrap my full lips around his hard dick.*

Passing his finger on my bottom lip and letting it linger, his eyes smoldering and dark, he took my fingers and placed them in his mouth. I watched as he kissed them and then he closed his eyes and sucked them. I watched in wonder. I felt a tingle move down my breasts and settle on my clit, then down to my toes. This type of foreplay was new to me. I felt intensely drawn to him, like metal drawn to a magnet. There was something sinful about how he kissed my fingers and then his lips found my mouth.

His tongue swirled around and sucked my tongue for as long as he'd sucked my fingers. I tried to reciprocate drawing in his tongue, but he was in control and sucked my mouth dry, determined to seduce me with his foreplay, and I was more than determined to allow him.

Lowering his head to my neck, he softly nipped it. The sensation was felt in my folds. His hands grabbed both breasts and his fingers squeezed my nipples, until they rose and ached with pleasure. His dark-green eyes searched my eyes as he lay over me, biting my neck and squeezing my nipples harder. I didn't cry out, because surprisingly, I enjoyed the intensity of his lovemaking. His gaze locked on me, and he saw in my eyes that I enjoyed every moment of his painful seduction.

"Does pain give you pleasure?" he asked meeting my gaze and his fingers tightening on my nipples. *Yes, how did he know? I just found out.*

"Yes, yes, harder," I moaned breathless. His eyes gleaming, he pinched my nipples harder. My breathing intensified.

His head moved down, his short curly locks brushing against my breasts. I threaded my fingers through his dark locks, as he sucked each nipple, careful to tug each one in his teeth, until they rose and turned red. I gave out a low moan. When I shouted it was with pleasure. He appeared hungry for a body, and that body lay in his bed, and it was mine.

I felt as if I had won the lottery. I was a lucky fuck for the day.

The compromise of my beliefs for that beautiful man making a meal out of my breasts, gorging himself until he felt satisfied, filled me with pleasure. He took them in his hands, "These are beautiful, I can't get enough of them..." he said, stroking them, pinching each nipple as they met his fingers. "...and they are mine." A dark gleam settled in his eyes, a penetrating look that made me want to pull the straps of the silk top down my hips, leaving the thong, a thin strip up my ass crack, masquerading as underwear.

He helped pull the top down, and looked on me with my breasts heaving up and down. He straddled me as his eyes searched every inch of my body, then he reached his large hands on both sides of the string, and with one jerk, the strings came undone, and his gaze lowered and settled on my pubic hair.

"Let it grow, don't shave it again," he demanded, then sliding down my body slowly, stopping to place a warm kiss on my stomach, his hands parted my legs, and he dropped his magnificent face between my legs. His tongue searched around my clit, until he found the spot he had been looking for. He caught me by surprise. My legs trembled, but soon relaxed and I opened them wide.

I carelessly draped my legs over his shoulder, which excited me as well as him, because he clutched them with both hands, never coming up for breath.

His head moved with the intensity and the rhythm of his tongue. I had wanted to know how it felt to have a man eat me. I had heard about it, but I didn't know it was so pleasurable. His energy was boundless. His hands cupped my breasts, and his fingers pinched my nipples as he worked his tongue. He had mastered a rhythm with his lips, tongue, hands, and fingers—the epitome of extreme multi-tasking.

I had my first orgasm, and before I could yell, I had another one. It was a terrific feeling, and I could not contain a scream of pleasure. With a smile on his face, he moved and eased his body up, gazing into my eyes. I took his dick into my hands, and he looked at me, his eyes begging me to do something with it, or to it. It was so hard when I took it into my mouth, lying on my back, I feared that my mouth could not contain it.

He saw the panic in my eyes; I didn't want to do the wrong thing, so I took it out. "I've never done this before," I said, looking up at Mr. Black.

"I know," he said softly.

*How does he know,* I asked myself? Now was not the time to analyze.

"I'll teach you. I'll teach you to satisfy me." Those words sounded promising. Maybe I wasn't a one-night stand after all, but I was certainly his cunt for the day. As he directed me to hold his warm dick in my hand, I clutched it gently. "No, you're holding it like you're afraid of it. Tighter."

Finally, I got it. I felt in control as he tilted his head back, moaning with pleasure, "Alex, yes, that's what I like. Now, suck it hard. I don't want to fill your mouth with my come. I want to fill your pussy. I can't wait."

With little patience, I sucked the head of his penis; up and down my mouth took it in. I wanted to control that dark, handsome, sexy, and titillating love of my life, man of my dreams, fucking trouble, who had ruined me for other men.

Tasting a hint of warm fluid, dropping slow, drip by drip, until he pulled his dick from my mouth, and he held it with a painful expression, then with his strong arms, he lifted me up facing him.

With his head buried in my breasts, he whispered, "Put it in Alex." I hesitated, my hands quivered at the thought of the pain his hot, wet penis would inflict on the walls of my vagina. I guided his hard penis to the entrance of my vagina and stopped. I glared at Mr. Black with panicked eyes. "You're a virgin, I know. I'll be careful." His mouth locked around my nipple, his long arm reaching, and his fingers finding my folds, sending a current shooting to my toes. He opened my wet folds and inserted a finger, then gently another finger, then breached my walls. Taking his fingers out, he placed them to his nose and inhaled, then inserted them into his mouth on his tongue, and said,

"It's your smell that turns me on. That smell tells me no man has been here."

Holding my breath, he plowed the tip of his heavy penis into my vagina, inch by inch, taking more of my opening, until he reached a roadblock, then with a quick thrust he filled my vagina, as if he had heard somewhere that to limit the pain and reach the summit of a mountain, he had to do it quickly.

The nerves of my clit came alive. Opening my mouth to scream, his mouth cupped my mouth, and he sucked my tongue in, rendering me speechless as he arched his body deep into my opening. I became used to his incredible hard penis. I took it in easily. It was a good fit. I knew it and he knew it.

Overmatched by his incredible body, his incredible lovemaking, his incredible handsome face, I yielded everything to him.

His energy was boundless. "I need more." He glanced across my body instead of looking into my eyes. I didn't say a word. I was numb from the meds, but I knew what I was doing and where I was going. He whispered, "I should have been gentle, but I couldn't help myself. Your virgin pussy was so sweet and irresistible." He looked like a child declaring that he could not resist a piece of candy.

Mr. Black's face softened, and enjoyment and pleasure took hold. I wanted to give him the pleasure of my body where he would never forget me. As he thrust his dick into me once more, I met it with enjoyment, as I tried to find out just what turned on my gorgeous fuck of a man. My fingernails trailed up and down his back, until I found that he responded, "Fuck me, Alex, never stop. I love you, you're mine, and I'm your first."

*And you will be my only man. I don't want anyone but you. Ever!* I thought.

Leaning his head back, his breathing intensified. I worked my hips at each positive expression on his face. His animalistic moans caused me to thrust forward into him, and milk his penis up and down with my tight cunt. His body shook violently with pleasure, and his come slowly drained into me.

He pulled me close, our eyes meeting as I lay with my head on his hard, muscular arm. I looked around and saw a large moon casting light on his hard chest. He knew all about me, but I knew nothing of him, except that I loved him, and he said that he loved me. I wanted to believe him.

Turning to face me with his hands between my thighs, he murmured, "Alex, you look so sexy. I want more of you." He nudged under me and stroked my behind. His gaze covered my body as he fought off sleep, but he wasn't successful, and sleep won out. I was too giddy to close my eyes. I just stared at him with his drop-dead gorgeous looks and body; his arm draped across my stomach. I wondered how I had gotten so lucky, then I realized that I had never been lucky. I turned, lying in his arms with my head on his chest, and I remained in a state of ignorant bliss.

# Chapter 2

W aking to a clear sky and scenery to die for, anxious to take a shower, I attempted to get up, when in walked a burly redheaded woman with her hair in a tight bun. "Ms. Bishop, I'm your nurse. Mr. Blackstone instructed me to bathe you, and not allow you to walk on that ankle," she stated like a drill sergeant.

"Yes, but where is Mr. Blackstone?" I questioned, my eyes searching around for my Mr. Black.

"Mr. Blackstone placed a letter on the night table with instructions for you to follow. He had meetings and then he's flying on to San Francisco."

"Did Mr. Blackstone say anything about returning to Montana?"

"He doesn't share that type of information with me, Ms. Bishop," she said, looming over me.

"Of course, he doesn't, you are the nurse, not his secretary," I said full of sarcasm, taking my anger out on someone, anyone. I felt used, but that could not be. "*We are all adults,*" Mr. Black had stated.

Glancing at the antique clock on the nightstand, my eyes settled on expensive stationery. The clock bonged out 9 a.m. Where had the time gone? Last thing I remembered, I was getting the fuck of my life, and lying in Max's arms. Now I was being ordered around by Broom-Hilda.

"Ms. Bishop... Ms. Bishop, pay attention," she said with a rise in her strong voice.

"Yes, yes, I heard you. You can help me into the shower."

"Then, we can go to the fitness room afterwards."

"Whatever you say," I mumbled, rolling my eyes. She assisted me as I limped into the shower, trying not to put my full weight on my ankle. I followed her directions in a daze, and agreed to a massage that almost killed me, but I was fit for the next day. Well, maybe my body, but my mind was a wreck.

After my shower, Hilda placed a luxurious white robe on the door, and I slipped it on. After placing me on the bed, a maid brought in two eggs sunny-side up, English muffin, imported strawberry jam, a pot of English Breakfast Tea and milk. Mr. Black knew what I liked for breakfast. I wondered what else he knew. But what did I know of him. For one, he was impossibly handsome, he liked oral sex, and he said that he loved me. I didn't need to know any more.

I sat for a moment, staring at the fancy envelope with his brand on the front. It was written in the most refined cursive script. My hands shook as I opened the folded page. It was so impersonal, I expected Dear Darling, something romantic, but it read:

*Dear Ms. Bishop,*

*I have had a most interesting and fortuitous night. It is with great pleasure that I make this admission. Never have I been so taken with a woman as with you. Never have I felt as intense as I have with any woman. Our act of lovemaking is embedded in my soul, and I can't forget you, nor do I want to allow you to have another man experience the pleasures I have come to enjoy.*

*Therefore, I am making an offer of employment at my head office in San Francisco, California. I assure you that you will not regret your decision. Furthermore, look over the contract that I have enclosed, then sign it and present it to my butler. He will see that the document reaches me immediately. Thank you for your time.*

*Mr. Maximilian Blackstone, Esq.*

After reading the letter, the hairs on the back of my neck rose. I sat up in the bed, murmuring, "I have never been so insulted in my life. What kind of man says to a woman he had a fortuitous night? Yes, it was fortuitous for you, Mr. Black. Who would have thought that I would have been so easy to be seduced, fucked within the inch of my life? Not me, and probably not him." I was a captive audience,

I rationalized, but who was I kidding; I wanted him so badly that I would have climbed a mountain if he told me to. Instead, I let him climb me and plant his flag.

There he was, tall, dark, and silent, but he spoke aloud with his body. That was his thing; he could make love to a woman like no other—not that I had anyone to compare it to—and then put her on the payroll, to ensure that he would have endless pussy.

*He's not going to get off that easy,* I vowed. I knew that I had an effect on him and he was trying to hide it from me. You would think he was too old to play games, but here he was treating me like a commodity. I took the letter and the contract in my hands, made a ball of it, then angrily threw it on the floor.

Anxious to get back to work and forget that hot fuck of my life, I needed to sleep away the day. I reached for the muscle relaxants that Dr. Watson, or whatever his name was, had prescribed, and I slept. I got up around midnight and limped out of bed and through the door. Seeing a light, I headed in that direction. Passing a bedroom, I stopped long enough to turn the knob longing to see my tall, dark, handsome drink of water come to greet me.

A faint light on a desk near a large California king bed provided a substantial view of the room. There were no pictures of naked women or anyone, no mother, brother, or sister. I guessed he used this room for sleeping, and the other for his orgies. My curiosity got the best of me, and I wobbled to the bed, slowly holding on to the edge until I reached the closet door, and opened it.

Someone said you could tell everything about a person by their closet, or was it their kitchen. I walked into it, and it was larger than a small house. There hung rows and rows of black suits and shoes, and more white shirts than I could count. There wasn't much color, and then I spied an array of silk ties providing just a hint of color. He had a large display of cufflinks, gold watches, and a display case of Montblanc pens.

His closet revealed nothing, only that he liked black, he was partial to order, and he had enough money to collect things. I didn't want to spend my time overanalyzing him, because I came to the realization that I was out of my class, so I turned to get the hell out of there, when a figure showed in the doorway.

"Can I assist you, Ms. Bishop?"

"I was looking for something to eat and my phone when I passed this room," I said, nervous and surprised.

"If you allow me to help you back to your room, the maid will bring you a midnight snack. "My name is Rodger Van Horn. I'm Mr. Blackstone's butler."

Looking up at Rodger, I placed my hand on his shoulder. I limped back to the room, looking in his face to determine how he viewed me. He was surprisingly handsome for a man of sixty. He appeared to have all of his whitish-blond hair. His face was etched with years of sun, and his manners were perfect.

"Your belongings are packed for you; if you decide to leave they will be given to you."

After I lay in the bed for a minute, he promptly brought a tray, laden with cold chicken sandwiches, and a choice of three beverages—water, beer, and a cola. "If you require some dessert, push that button and someone will attend to your needs."

He reached the door and turned. "The house phone is in that drawer," he said, pointing to the night stand. "Just hit that button and it will appear."

I swallowed the sandwich and washed it down with a bottle of Heineken beer. I had no intentions of staying any longer than I had to. I found the phone and called Joshua."

"Hello."

"Joshua."

"Who is this?"

"It's me. Alex."

"Alex, where the hell are you? I thought something had happened to you, because I didn't hear from you and you didn't show for work."

"You have to find the address of Blackstone's home, it's somewhere near the Lodge. It's a large cabin setting atop a mountain. Someone at work must have the address. Come get me when you finish your shift tomorrow."

"Why are you whispering? Did that freak kidnap you? Did he do something to you?"

"Come on, Joshua, it's not as dramatic as you think. I'll tell you everything, just come get me."

Sleep didn't come easy, but I managed to get a few hours. The next morning, I had been under the care of Mr. Black for two days, and you would think that he would have called me. I gave him a chance, but he never called, not even to check on my leg.

After climbing out of my lover's bed, I was walking normally. I'm sure Broom-Hilda was the major cause, plus the muscle relaxant that I used as a sleeping aid to forget Mr. Black. I was dressed in my ski suit before the maid entered.

"No, Miss, Mr. Blackstone gave you these clothes. She opened the closet, and dresses and suits were lined up, dresses costing thousands of dollars. I glanced at one dress, and thought, *When did these get here? Where will I ever wear this?* It was a Hervé Léger bandage dress, and the price tag had two thousand stamped on it, and the next dress was even higher. The thought made me feel sick.

*Who does he think I am? He can't buy me. I fell in love with that man, and this is how he treats me. I want nothing from him, not even his love,* I declared in a fit of anger. I walked away in silence with not even my dignity, and sat in the chairs waiting for Joshua. No sooner had I sat down when Roger handed me the crumpled letter and contract. "I doubt that you have read this, Miss," he stated, looking down on me. I never met his gaze.

I took it to be polite, and stuffed it into my pocket. He left in the direction of the bedrooms. Joshua's Volvo pulled up, and I stood waving from inside. It was forty degrees and light snow blanketed the roads.

"What's wrong, Alex?" Joshua said with a mixture of concern and anger. With his help I got into his dark-gray Volvo, he closed the door, and padded around to the driver's seat, then drove in the direction of his apartment. A long silence settled on us, until I could no longer hide my anger and hurt.

"What did he see in me?" I questioned with tears welling in my eyes.

"A piece of ass," Joshua carelessly stated, as if conversing with one of his male buddies.

"Yes, I know, but a girl can dream," I said, peering at Joshua, who never took his eyes off the snow-covered road. "I'm not stupid. I know it was a dream until... until." It became impossible to finish. I sucked in air.

"Until what? Don't keep me on edge. Tell me."

"Until he made love to me and then he left, and I haven't heard from him. He left me alone in that mansion with his servants, and tried to pay me off with expensive clothes and another job."

"You should have taken them," he said, glancing at me with his big brown eyes.

"Then, that would make me a..."

"A whore?" he questioned, glancing at me after taking his eyes off the road.

"Watch what you're doing." I chastised.

"I want nothing from him. You should read that letter he left, and he had the nerve to enclose a contract. I crumpled it and threw it on the floor, but his butler retrieved it and gave it back and I shoved it in my pocket. I'll read it when I am able to stand thinking of him." I laid my head on Joshua's shoulder."

"You know people are whispering about you at work, Alex."

"What are they saying?" I raised my head, turning to face Joshua.

"The usually stuff." He paused, catching my gaze. "That you threw yourself at that rich cunt. Those are my words. I hate that rich bastard for making you so unhappy."

"I'll be alright as soon as I return to Brooklyn."

"You're not leaving, Alex?"

"I have to go."

"But what will you do for money?"

"Blackstone Enterprises gave me a generous package. I was paid fifty thousand dollars." Joshua hit the brakes and the car jerked and skidded. "Are you crazy?" I shouted.

"You were paid fifty thousand dollars for three months, and nothing about that offer rang a bell."

"I had to submit to an extensive background check, have a complete exam by the company's doctors. I needed the money, so I signed the contract."

"You're getting fifty thousand dollars for three months' work." He put the car in drive still staring at me.

"I know that was excessive, but I told the recruiter that I needed to pay my student loans. I would have agreed to anything."

"It appears you did agree to anything, but what? You didn't read the contract. Where is it?

"I don't know. I have it somewhere." I gave him a blank look, and he shook his head. "What are you saying, Joshua?"

"Why do you think that rich bastard asked about you? He already had you in his crosshairs. He picked you out from a picture and a binder, and you were delivered to him on a platter."

"Do you think I haven't thought of that? But the way you put it, it sounds obscene."

"You were used. Get over it."

"We were both used. I used his money and..." I stopped, because I had lost my virginity, my self-respect.

"He has more money than you can spend. He can buy more virgins," Joshua said, not taking his eyes off the road. He didn't know that I hated him at that moment for telling me the truth. They would always shoot the messenger.

We finally reached his apartment—a row of small buildings with two stories, all with balconies, where you could enjoy the stream running below, and the sun peeking from behind clouds and mountaintops on special occasions.

This was a time I needed some warmth, someone to talk to. I had to try to forget that tall, dark, handsome drink of water. I fell into the chair, my eyes following the river as it snaked up and down, taking pebbles with it. I compared myself to a stream and Max was the ocean. I moved around, twisting and turning, as if heading for the ocean. All rivers would eventually flow into oceans.

Anger got the best of me. I made up my mind to quit my job, forget Max and return to Brooklyn. I had to tell Joshua. He walked through the terrace doors, carrying a bottle of wine and two glasses. "Here, this will make you feel better."

I took a sip of wine. "I'm leaving for Brooklyn this week."

"Why Alex? You're going to let that bastard run you out of Montana."

"It's beautiful here, but I'm a city girl. I wasn't planning on staying long anyway."

"What are you going to do?"

"I paid off my college loans and I plan on racking up a fresh set. I'm going back to school. After that, I'll figure something out."

"But where are you going to live?"

"With the money I saved, and I sublet my apartment. I have no worries but one, well, maybe two." I gave Joshua a sheepish grin, and hunched my shoulders. He knew the wine would loosen my lips.

"Well."

"I had unprotected sex."

"Oh no, you didn't." Joshua stood up and walked around in a circle, more worried than me.

"I was caught up with that handsome gorgeous soft-spoken man."

"I'd say it was his handsome gorgeous hard dick."

"Well, that too." I tried to make light of it, and managed a small smile.

"I don't think he has a disease, but that was fucking irresponsible on his part. He's fucking thirty-five, an old man," Joshua went on, railing about Max's irresponsibility to me.

"It could be something worse."

"What could be worse, Alex?"

"I could be pregnant."

# Chapter 3

Three years had passed, and my life had changed. I grew up, no longer a novice or a sex-starved idiot.

A year into my master's program, Joshua texted me, implying he needed a vacation away from Montana. When I didn't answer, he e-mailed me, begging for a tour of Manhattan, promising that he would only stay a week. My whole life had been sucked up with school and life, and I needed a break too.

Joshua received a raise and the position of general manager of Blackstone Lodges and Hotels; I guessed he felt he had to celebrate. I met him at LaGuardia airport on a Friday evening, and a cab took us to Brooklyn to my apartment. After he settled in and looked around, he appeared pleased, because it was neat and clean. However, he found the apartment a little too small for his taste, but he was getting use to the idea and the people.

He walked into my room at eight o'clock the next morning, and sat on a bench at the foot of my bed.

"Do you always sleep that late?"

"No, but today is Saturday, and I don't plan to get up until eleven." Out of the clear blue sky he dropped this on me.

"Two days after you left, Blackstone came looking for you."

My heart raced as Joshua took his time torturing me. "He asked me questions about you, but I didn't tell him where you were. He tried giving me the position I have now, just so I would tell him where you had gone, but I told him I had no idea. Alex, when he didn't find you, he looked lost, and he sat in the bar for hours alone, just drinking."

"Not too lost. The next week I read an online San Francisco newspaper of his engagement to a debutante. I see he likes them young and stupid." I peered at Joshua with my heart broken, and not wanting an answer to the next question. "Did he marry her?"

"Why are you doing this to yourself? I thought that you never wanted to see him again?"

"Just answer my question, Josh." *I looked in his face begging him to lie to me. Tell me any lie I could stand. Tell me he didn't marry that silly girl. Tell me he would never marry until he found me, and that he said he could not breathe until he laid eyes on me, and when he found me he would go on his knees and beg me for my hand in marriage.*

Joshua only said, "No, he didn't marry her, but..."

"But what?" I said, exasperated with the way Joshua would tell a story. He would draw everything out and then pause, keeping me on edge.

"Now he's seeing this woman, she's about his age. Thirty-two, very rich in her own right."

"He's nothing but trouble, Alex."

I knew he was trouble, but then so was I. *My life is a series of troubling relationships with my parents and the disappointments,* I thought, staring at my hands.

"Then why did you go to bed with him? You're sensible. You're the most sensible girl I know," Joshua said, looking up from behind his Saturday New York Times.

"I couldn't resist his devilish smile, and I couldn't resist him, and besides, I fell in love with him... I have something else to tell you. I'm going to work in his office in San Francisco," I said, breaking the news.

"What? When?" Joshua said, stunned. "Do you know what you're doing? You're leaving New York to go to San Francisco, to languish in that dull climate where the Golden Gate Bridge is the only place to commit suicide. So, when he uses you the way he wants, and discards your ass after he has plundered it, then you have no choice but to end it all."

"No, I don't know what I'm doing." My gaze searched outside the picture window, settling on cars traveling down Ocean Avenue, eventually meeting Joshua's gaze. "He doesn't know what he has unleashed by his actions. He doesn't know who I am. There was an ad, and I answered it. His office in Manhattan hired me just like that. I changed my name to protect the innocent and the rest is history."

"I don't know who you are." We locked eyes. "Why are you doing this?"

I thought a minute. "For revenge. Revenge is a dish best served cold," I said, getting to my feet.

"You're in school; you need to give yourself a chance. You're too smart for what I see happening to you," Joshua said as he lifted himself from his usual position in front of his computer, taking a few minutes to get a cup of coffee. As he strolled by, he placed a soft tap on my forehead with the sports section of the paper. "You have never had a boyfriend, and Mr. Black and Freddie don't count," he continued, as if reading my mind and filling in the blank spaces.

"This is a treacherous job market. Just read the business section of the Times." I passed Joshua, who by now was enjoying his second cup of Green Mountain Coffee, minus sugar, snatching the paper from his hand, trying to get his attention. "And Freddie *does* count."

"You know nothing about that company. You know nothing about Mr. Black. What's their business model?"

"Blackstone Enterprises owns hotels. I have a job, and that's all I care about."

"You have always been a level-headed girl, and now you tell me that you are going halfway across the country, to work in a business that you don't have a notion of what they do. Well, then what are your duties?"

"I'll find out when I get there. I was told that I would be one of Mr. Blackstone's assistants, and I know enough about Mr. Black. He's a man and he has a weakness for virgins."

"To which you are no longer a member of that club."

"Fuck you, Joshua."

"When? I've been waiting for you."

"Try getting serious." I continued my analysis of Mr. Black. "His strengths are his weakness. He finds a virgin and then he is on to something else. Look at his dating card, debutantes and young girls. I wonder what else is lurking in his past."

"Look here. I've just googled him." Joshua smiled.

I rushed over leaning over Joshua's shoulder, reading the headlines: "*Maximilian Blackstone one of the most eligible bachelors in the U. S. or the world, and I bet he will stay a bachelor,*" I said adding commentary. "*He's worth billions with money from banking, hotels, minerals, oil, and inheritances.* That's his weakness—all that money, he's young and hot, and I bet he gets up every morning with a hard dick."

Joshua's brow furrowed, "Who are you?"

"Mr. Black's worst nightmare—a scorned young woman, who will exact my revenge from his beautiful ass." Sinking next to Joshua, staring into oblivion, I shook my head, having second thoughts. "What have I got myself into? Do you think I can do this?" I whispered.

"Didn't I just ask the same thing, remember?" Joshua said with a sarcastic smile and a tilt of his head.

Opening my Dell to check my e-mail, there was a reminder in my inbox.

*Re: Work Schedule at Blackstone Enterprises*

*Greetings, Ms. Bishop,*

*Mr. Blackstone expects you on Monday, in his office on time, and dressed appropriate for your first day. If you have a problem reaching your destination, a jet and limo have been made available for your convenience. Contact Blackstone Leer Jets at: 212- 3840478 and reserve your seat from New York to San Francisco. Mr. Blackstone is looking forward to having you as part of our family.*

Speechless, I motioned to Joshua, waving my hand feverishly in the air. I couldn't believe what I had just read.

"I'm impressed," Joshua said.

"Is that all you can say?"

"How do you plan on pulling this off?"

Giving Joshua a light smirk, I walked into my tiny closet, taking out a box with a blonde wig, then pulling it over my auburn hair, and slipping on my brown contacts. "What do you think?"

"Do you think that's going to fool him?" Joshua questioned.

"I don't think he even remembers what I look like."

"Why don't you come back to Montana and marry me. I make a good living." Joshua grabbed my hand, but I stole it back.

"But I don't love you. But I do... but not the way you want, Joshua."

"Yes, I want you to fuck me like you fucked Mr. Black, and then trail across the country to get even with me."

"Shut up." I got up from the chair and swatted Jacob across his forehead head with the business section of the Times.

"Today is Saturday, and you have to be in San Francisco by Monday, and get an apartment."

"Oh, shit," I said, raising my hand to my mouth. "I forgot about that. I can't pay for an apartment just like that in San Francisco. It's like living in Manhattan, the rent is outrageous. What am I going to do? What was I thinking?"

"Don't ask me."

"I have to get the hell out of Brooklyn before I lose my mind, Joshua. Now, help me pack. I didn't realize that I had to be there that soon. I guess I was so excited about the job that I forgot. I have too much on my mind," I said, pulling at my hair and biting my fingernails, which had turn into nubs, because of school and life. "I hate reading the small print."

I walked to my bed in the corner of my studio apartment. Under the bed, I had my belongings in a box—my degree, greeting cards from friends, some photos, a watch with an inscription from my father, and a pearl ring that belonged to my mother.

After pulling a shoe box out, sitting on the bed and rummaging through it, I found a folded paper with several pages. It looked like a contract. It *was* a contract. This was the first time I had taken a good look at it.

After reading a few lines, I looked up. "Do you believe this?"

"What? What?" Joshua said, lifting his head from his computer.

"I can't believe I signed this and didn't read it."

"And you want to be a lawyer? What's in it?" Joshua said, studying my changing expressions, wrestling the paper from my hands.

We both read it aloud.

*Ms. Johns agrees to perform duties as designated by Mr. Blackstone, to be decided and expressed on each day that she is employed at his company. If she agrees and signs this contract, then she is bound by the stipulations. Once she has signed the contract, she cannot be released from it without penalty of law.*

"Well, that was short and sweet. He's a man of few words, and you didn't take time to read this? What's on the next pages?" Joshua turned to the next page. There was a picture of the uniform. It was a picture of a black suit and a white shirt.

"Well, I have that."

"Well, I bet you don't. Can't you see that's a Versace suit, and a white Carolina Herrera shirt. The shirt alone costs a thousand dollars? If you have time to shop, which you don't, and if you have money to buy it, which you don't..."

"Shut the fuck up, Joshua, you are so negative. I'll buy a knockoff."

"You don't have money even for a knockoff. Look, sweetheart, I'm being realistic. You're in way over your head."

"I need this job. I have no choice. All I have is a college degree, college debt, and you." I laid my head on his shoulder, and he laid his head on mine. "I'll fake it," I said.

"All I have is you, and you are leaving me." Tears welled in our eyes. There was a ding coming from Joshua's computer. He had an e-mail.

"Oh no... I'm going to San Francisco with you to open up this new hotel."

We were dancing around in circles. "Now I can keep my eye on you."

"I don't need a babysitter," I shot back.

"You need something."

"Yes, some money."

"I have a little. You know there's a rider attached to this contract. Do you want me to read it?"

"No. I don't want to be depressed, and I don't want to hear what you have to say today. I'll read it later. I've committed myself already. Knowing more will only make me upset."

"You will never read this until you have to," Joshua said, staring me down. "Oh, well." He threw the contract back in my shoe box, saying, "Procrastinator."

# Chapter 4

W e stepped off Blackstone's private jet, in cloudy fog-ridden San Francisco. A limo driver sent a text to Joshua, we quickly found him, and we were off to our destination. I tagged along with him. After all, he was the executive, and I was promised a job editing a newsletter, and writing pieces for Blackstone's online publications, to promote oil drilling.

Stopping at the door of a luxurious apartment with the Golden Gate Bridge as part of the scenery, our bags were handed to the doorman, and he quickly placed them in the apartment before we reached the eighth floor. The carpet, lush, and high, lined the Italian marble walkway, glowed throughout the building. Incredible. Joshua's gaze wandered, and he said, "I can get used to this—an apartment, six-figure income to manage Blackstone's properties, and all because I know you."

"What do you mean?"

"The only reason Blackstone gave me a large salary, is because he hopes I will tell him something about you."

"He probably forgot about me. Well, I sure hope he has, because it will make it much easier to do what I need to do," I said with a weak heart.

Walking through the apartment; there were two bedrooms, which were perfect, modern furniture, no antiques. I fell across the bed, and could not move and fell asleep, because of the time change. I woke the next day, and we decided to go for a walk to see the city. We needed some coffee, and straggled into the nearest pub which was open all hours selling cappuccino, a drink with chocolate, brandy, and steamed milk, served in the mornings, and by night, you could get a good dark beer and a Manhattan.

Plopping down in a booth in the corner of the restaurant, suddenly a pair of green eyes attached to a familiar handsome face turned in our direction. I hit Joshua on the arm. "He's coming this way," I whispered.

"Who?" a reflex action took over, and Joshua raised his menu in front of his face.

Before I could leave the booth and tell Joshua that our boss was standing in front of us, I was facing him. "Excuse me, but I think I know you from somewhere."

*Yes, you, love of my life, you rich handsome fuck, who buried your face between my legs, and left me with the taste of your dick in my mouth, and fucked me every which way but loose. You treated me like a whore; yes, you do know me, you sexy bastard.* I wanted to say all those things, but I didn't. "I'm sorry, I've never met you." I smiled, flicking my pony tail, lowering my eyes, sitting, and slumping into my seat. He never looked at Joshua, because Joshua had his head turned to the wall with the menu covering his face.

"I would like to speak to you when you're alone."

"I'm very seldom alone?"

"I see that you're not married."

"And what makes you come to such a hasty conclusion?"

"You're not wearing a wedding ring, or an engagement ring," he countered.

"Well, are you a detective or a serial killer?" He shook his head, tilting it to the side and smiled.

"Neither." His sparkling green eyes glowed, and then he let out a wonderful, subdued laugh. I hadn't seen that side of him. He knew how to take a joke.

*Let's see how he handles the joke I'm getting ready to play on him.*

"Here's my card," he stated, trying to meet my diverted gaze. "I'll be waiting for your call." I looked up. He held the card out, staring into my eyes, as if he could put me in a trance.

I had been in his trance from the first moment I met him, and clearly I still was, because I took the card from his hand. He had accomplished what he wanted. Turning, he strode back to his booth, then out through the door with a man who had been waiting at the bar. No doubt a bodyguard.

Through the picture window I saw an attendant standing in front of an exotic silver sports car with the door ajar. My Mr. Black, the fuck of my life, my sexual mentor, slipped into it with ease, and drove off.

"Did you see that? He not only didn't remember me, he was after another conquest with the same person. He can't remember the women he seduced and screwed." I sat brimming with anger, hitting the spoon on the table, wishing I had slapped his face instead.

"I couldn't see anything but that two-point-five-million-dollar Bagatti," Joshua noted in awe. He paused giving in to a moment of hero worshiping. "Alex, if you don't do this right, you could cost me my position and my job with Blackstone Industries, and I like this job. You will have to assume your other persona, and please tell me, I don't need surprises. I have to commit that to memory and all the other bullshit you are planning. I'm a part of this nonsense now."

"It may be nonsense to you, but I need to do this. He likes fast cars. And how did you know that car cost two point five million? I wonder if he likes fast women," I said, passing my finger over my cheek, studying the possibilities.

"That car was in the New York Times. Alex, there's talk among the employees that he's into Bondage and S&M. What are you hoping to accomplish? He could be dangerous. Men with that kind of money and sex habits are dangerous."

"What do you know about BDSM, Josh?"

"About as much as you."

"I need to do this Josh. I want him to hurt like I have."

"If he's into bondage, then you will hurt more than him. A powerful rich man is seldom out of control, so watch your ass." Joshua laughed with relish at his own words.

"From my limited knowledge of BDSM, I read that once he penetrated me, he could not come back for more. But he did come back again and again in one night, and he bonded with me, and tried to erase the bond by staying away."

Joshua listened with interest, leaning in to capture every word. "You appear to be serious about that BDSM thing. Are you sure you want to cross that line? Remember, when you dig one grave for someone, dig one for yourself," Joshua said, staring me down.

"Yes, I'm crossing that line," I stated with a lack of reservation. "You know about Alexander Bishop, now it's time for you to get you acquainted with Ms. Rebecca Johns. She's a bleached blonde specializing in BDSM. And on her day off she wears tight seductive clothes, where she enjoys receiving and giving pain. I haven't decided whether I am the Dom or sub, but that will come later. Her family lives in Washington State, however, she previously resided in upstate New York, is a college graduate, and was hired by the personnel department in one of Blackstone's companies in New York City. We met on Blackstone's Leer Jet, and you invited me to share an apartment with you. You are not privy to my extracurricular activities." Joshua raised an eyebrow. "I'm trying to protect you, my friend."

Rolling his eyes and shaking his head, he said, "Anything else I should know? And what do you know about bondage?"

"What I don't know, I can learn."

"You already have a full-time job, or have you forgotten that."

"Yes, my full-time job is getting that handsome beautiful sick fuck to fall passionately in love with Rebecca. I want to drive him mad. I want him to obsess behind me until he loses his mind."

"Be careful what you wish for," Joshua said, laughing.

The clock beeped at 6 a.m. Monday, I dressed early to get a good start, where I could become acclimated to the city. Checking the city map, to my surprise, the main office of Blackstone Enterprises was within walking distance from the apartment.

Dressed in a black knockoff designer suit, and a white shirt with cuffs, a string of white pearls, a pair of black designer pumps, and an expensive black Prada purse that cost a fortune, I felt like a million dollars. In a briefcase I concealed my black six-inch pumps. I set out for my first day on the job with knots in my stomach. Strolling to the glass silver structure with Blackstone emblazoned over the entrance, I lumbered through the door, turning in circles, stopping to look up at the large chandeliers hanging in the lobby.

*Incredible,* I thought.

After taking a few steps, the elevator opened and out strutted my Mr. Black, carrying a black briefcase and a phone firmly in his hand. He obviously had a meeting, because he had on his signature black suit with white shirt and his prep school tie. I looked at his feet and he was without his Gucci loafers. Instead, he wore a pair of bespoke black Italian leather shoes.

When I raised my head, he paused, then he turned in my direction, continuing his conversation with his eyes, appraising and scanning my body. His expression signaled, *Where have I seen you? And I want to fuck you.* The elevator slowed, easing to a stop.

I stood staring him down. My face and eyes said, *"Whatever you want, I'm here to give it to you."*

Discovering I could hide the real me under a blonde wig, false eyelashes, makeup, and moderately expensive clothing, set me free. I could be who I wanted. Maybe I wasn't Alex. Maybe I was someone else.

Seducing him with a devilish smile, showing no teeth, watching him breathing hard, then turning my back to him facing the elevator, and feeling his burning stare, turning around, I flashed a wink and a full

smile. By the way he stood in that one spot, I knew he was mine. The elevator came, I stepped in, and his bodyguard touched his arm. I could see that Mr. Black was annoyed at the closing of the elevator door.

His hungry yearning green eyes spelled danger, but I wouldn't heed the signs, and I plowed straight ahead with my plans. When I reached the twenty-sixth floor, which took only a few seconds, I got off with my ears ringing and my head swirling.

"Hi, and you are?" I gave my papers to the pretty secretary at the front desk. She glanced up at me, lifting her eyebrows, and twisting her pretty face with suspicion and contempt. "Please, come with me, Miss Johns." She walked me through another set of doors with a guard sitting at the desk. Waving at him, he allowed us to go on to another section. "This is your office Ms. Johns, your secretary will be in to acquaint you with your duties."

My secretary? Well, no one said that I would have a secretary. The young woman about twenty-two, black hair and blue eyes, turned around looking in my eyes, "If you need to speak to Mr. Blackstone, you can relate the message to me, or your secretary. My name is Ms. Corday." And she turned coldly in her high heels and headed in the direction of her desk.

"Hmm. That will be the day," I murmured.

A woman of forty came into my office. She knew her place, and she appeared to have no feelings about me or Mr. Black. Perhaps she had no inclinations or desires for him, which was not so obvious with the young woman who sat at the welcome desk. She appeared to have had a piece of him, and wanted more.

It had taken my secretary the whole day to explain my duties, which were research and editing reports on the various entities of Blackstone Industries. Once I completed each binder, I had to hand it over to my secretary, and she would edit it as well. It was a secluded job, not tiring, but no contact with others. My lunch was controlled, because it was brought in. At four I heard footsteps, and someone entering the large

office attached to mine. After fifteen minutes, a knock came to the door, and without a word, Mr. Black strutted into my office.

Sitting behind my desk, head lowered glancing over tomorrow's assignment, I glanced up, and there stood my Mr. Black, so handsome, so exciting, and so fuckable. "Ms. Johns, I am..."

"I know who you are, sir. You are my employer, Mr. Blackstone," I said with my professional voice, trying to determine if he wanted a Dom or sub. I stood and walked to shake his hand as stern and hard as I could, not with the wimpy handshake I wanted to give him.

"You have a strong handshake."

"Thank you. I like when a man can appreciate a strong handshake from a woman."

"It shows that she likes to be in charge," he said with a sexy smirk, causing dimples to make a large dent in his cheeks.

*Oh, that told me everything. He wants a Dom, or is he just testing me?*

"I was hoping you would join me for dinner." He threaded his fingers through his tempting curly locks. Remembering the day I threaded my fingers through his hair, gave me a tingle between my legs.

"Do you have a habit of taking your help to dinner?"

"Only if they are as attractive and sexy as you."

"Mr. Blackstone, that can be construed as sexual harassment."

"Go ahead, sue me. I can afford it." He smiled, then it turned into a sly mischievous grin. "I assure you, you will have a better time if you just agree to have dinner with me."

*He's a persistent bastard when he wants something. I guess that's why he's a billionaire,* I thought. "I'm sorry Mr. Blackstone, but I have a previous engagement."

I walked around to my desk to take off my heels and put on my walking shoes. Bending down changing my shoes, I heard him say, "Did you read the rider and the fine print on the contract?" He turned and disappeared without saying more. I bit my nails, which didn't have the same effect as biting my real nails. At least he didn't press me further.

*Who reads the fine print on contracts,* I thought. *Not me. Not me.* I heard his office door open and close, and I began packing my company's iPad and iPhone.

Closing my door, I headed for the elevators. They finally stopped on the ground level, and I rushed for the revolving door. I saw a Midnight Blue Rolls Royce sitting in front at the curb, with Mr. Black leaning on his door with his legs crossed, wearing a dark-blue turtle neck, with dark slacks hanging perfectly on his glorious hips, held up with an alligator belt, and those Gucci loafers on his feet. He had plans for me, and I hadn't thought enough ahead to outwit this shrewd handsome fuck. After all, it was my first day, couldn't he give me a break?

"You look tired and hungry, Ms. Johns, would you like a ride home?"

"I live around the corner. I can find my way. Thank you, Mr. Blackstone, but I have a date." I started walking and he followed me. His driver drove off. The street was a one way, and we were headed in the opposite direction.

He paused, then asked, "Do you have a date with a young man?"

"No, with an old man. I like them old." I raised my eyebrow and gave him a wink.

"Like me?" he asked, stopping me with a slight grasp of my arm.

"No, you're too young." His brow furrowed, he didn't want to continue, so he changed the subject.

"You shouldn't walk alone."

I looked up at him and said, "I'm not alone."

He smiled and I saw an ease and warmth brush his strong clean-shaven, handsome face. I felt the warmth ease through my body, the way I saw him when he gazed into my eyes and said that he loved me. Was that his usual rap for all the virgins he deflowered? I couldn't have been the only one that he professed love for, but I would like to think that I was.

"A penny for your thoughts, Ms. Johns."

"Only a penny, Mr. Blackstone?"

"How about if I make it more and put it in your pay."

"I still wouldn't tell you what I'm thinking. A body needs some privacy. Besides, you can't bribe me." I glanced up at the building, and announced, "I'm home."

"If I remember precisely, this is one of my apartments."

The sign read Blackstone Apartments in LED lights. "One of your hotel managers is my roommate."

"A male or female?"

"A male."

"Is he your lover?"

"I don't think this is an appropriate conversation, and I don't care to explain to you, Mr. Blackstone." A smile crossed his face. He was as much surprised as I was at my words.

"Call me Max."

"Well, Max, thank you for walking me home." I extended my hand, and he pressed his face next to mine and our lips found each other, and there we stood outside kissing like teenagers. A hot kiss seared my lips. His tongue sliced through my mouth, so I sucked it in and began sucking it hard. His breathing accelerated and I felt his heart, and I knew he was attracted to Rebecca, the way he had been attracted to Alex three years ago.

I felt Mr. Black's hands bring me into his hard muscular body; I felt the flex of his muscular arms pressing me closer and closer. I felt him; all of him, rise and pulsate against my warm vagina. I smelled his scent, there was nothing like the smell of Tom Ford's Noir fragrance to make you lose all your inhibitions. I couldn't help myself.

Limp, and a moment from fainting in his arms, I got control of myself, but his hands had moved from my waist to my behind. He wasn't surprised that I allowed so much familiarity without protest. He acted as if he expected it.

With one hand behind my back, he whispered in my ear, "I want to smell your pussy. I need that and I need to be your slave."

He took my virginity and taught me about oral sex, now he was preparing me for BDSM.

*I wonder what's next?*

From my limited knowledge of BDSM, he was not supposed to kiss me or get personally involved if he was the Dom. He did say he wanted to be my slave. I smiled at the thought.

"I need to go; I'll see you tomorrow, Mr. Blackstone." Prying my body from his arms, I strutted away from him, and through the large glass door. I didn't turn until I reached the elevators. Swiveling around on my low heels, he was standing looking at me like a sex-starved schoolboy. A sly smile crossed his face, and he tilted his head to the side, then strode in the direction of his Rolls. The chauffer opened the door, and he glided in.

I didn't want him taking the role of gentleman, which he had initiated when first I met him. Then he could do what he wanted, and I would be left wishing and wanting him to call. This time would be different.

Opening the door to our apartment, I couldn't wait to tell Joshua. "Where are you, Joshua?" I searched around in his bedroom, in the kitchen, and finally the terrace. He had a glass of wine in his hand, and another empty glass waiting for me. "Pour me one. I have something to tell you."

"Do you see that bridge?" he said, words slurring. "I'm going to commit suicide if you fuck this up, Alex. I'm getting inquiries already about our relationship."

"Already? I just left Mr. Black," I said, surprised by the news and surprised by Joshua's misplaced concerns.

"This morning, at the new hotel, I saw him whispering to someone, then he came over and spoke to me. His voice was cold and stern when he asked about you, I mean Rebecca. I can't keep all those names in my head. I thought he was asking about you, Alex, the real you, not that blonde slut you're pretending to be."

"Well, what happened, Joshua? You never tell a straight story."

"He asked if I was fucking you. Just like that. I didn't expect that, especially from a man in his position. What have you done to him?"

"He's a man and he's into me. Things are about to get interesting."

"Alex, do you know that you have a clause in your employment that has something to do with BDSM. You need to know what you're in for." I rolled my eyes. "I don't think you are aware of what is expected from that job."

"I can handle it. What could be wrong with a little dirty talk with your dream man, and a little sex? It's not like it's new to me. Don't worry."

"You're in uncharted waters, Alex."

Taking time to read the fine print, I thought nothing of it. He expected to have a little dirty talk and BDSM. I knew a little of BDSM, I googled it. Besides, it didn't matter. I would be doing it with the love of my life. I figured that I could talk dirty with Blackstone, and I would have the last laugh when I confronted him with the truth.

# Chapter 5

I arrived in my office on Tuesday to find a note setting on my desk under a crystal paperweight. *He likes to write these damn notes,* I thought.

*Ms. Johns, Please, see me in my office at your earliest* convenience. *There is a matter that I would very much like to speak to you about. It needs your prompt attention.*

*Max*

I couldn't imagine what he could possibly have to discuss with me this early in the morning. I would just ignore it. I took the note and balled it up and threw it into an obscenely expensive garbage bin sitting near my desk. Plopping down on the white leather chair, swiveling around and around, trying to acclimate myself to the wonderful surroundings and scenery that begged for a second look, I stood, walked to the floor-to-ceiling window, and leaned on it, taking in the landmarks that San Francisco was famous for.

I turned my head, searching around, trying to see Alcatraz. Suddenly, I remembered that I had to read the fine print on that contract I had signed previously for Blackstone. Reaching for my purse, I found the contract, scanning it I glanced at a paragraph that had me breathless, "Oh my God. Does he expect me to do this?" Putting my finger to my lip, *Isn't this illegal?* I thought.

"Not between consenting adults. Not if I signed this iron-clad contract with a disclaimer." I was more than pissed now. I decided to take my time, why should I rush? Now I had an idea of what he expected from his assistants, so I turned on my iPhone only to receive a text message.

MONDAY 12, 2013

*Max: Rebecca, I need u now. Don't make me beg.*

I placed my hand over my mouth to muffle my laugh. "Well, I'll give him something to think about. I can't believe he wants dirty talk early in the morning." So, I sent him an answer.

*Becky: Mr. Blackstone, I'm busy pleasuring myself. My pussy is hot and wet and can't wait for u.*

*Max: U shouldn't breach your contract. I warn u, I'm a lawyer as well. I should have the opportunity to provide appropriate toys for you. How do you feel about a dildo in Ur cunt, and my dick in your ass?*

*Becky: I want the real thing in my pussy and put the dildo in my ass. How do you feel about me sucking your hard cock?*

*Max: U R aware a SUB does not initiate that act unless it is requested by the DOM.*

*Becky: U R aware that U can throw away the BDSM manual and let Ur self-go. Try eating my pussy, for example. I won't tell anyone.*

*Max: I know what you need, a light spanking, and my shaft in your ass.*

*Becky: I know what you need, my pussy in your mouth.*

*Max: I don't know how I can resist that offer. I'll be in your office in seconds; I hope you are ready for your second day on the job.*

I heard a door slam, and listened as he informed my secretary that he didn't want to be disturbed. He stood in my office with his hands behind him, where the sound of the click of a lock reverberated, making a distinct sound.

His eyes blazed with need. He pulled his expensive alligator belt from his gray slacks, and tied it around his neck like a dog collar. It shocked me at first, but I tried not to show any expression. After all, I had signed the contract stating that I had experience with BDSM, and it was among my job description. He said nothing, then pulled his deep maroon-colored V-neck silk sweater over his head, showing his biceps, six pack, and a deep tan. His hard muscles rippled, and when he moved his arms to take off his shoes, the muscles in his arms flexed into hard rocks.

He then removed his slacks and underwear, standing naked with his large penis jutting out. "I lay myself bare for you. I've never been taken by a woman as much as I'm taken by you."

I didn't want to hear those words; those words were for Alex, not slutty Rebecca. For that I was determined to make him pay. "Get to your knees," I said, as he kneeled with his eyes never leaving me. Finally, I felt my power. *I may get use to this*, I thought.

I couldn't believe that I was commanding this handsome billionaire to do my bidding.

He stayed on his knees looking up at me. I walked from around my desk wearing a pair of six-inch black heels with red soles. His eyes followed my feet, and I saw his mouth water and his Adam's apple move. Standing in front of him, I asked, "How much do you want me?"

"I want you so much, feel me. I'm just about to come looking at you."

"You will not come until I command you to. What will you do to have me control you?"

"Anything you want?" he said, gazing up at me standing over him with my legs opened wide.

I took off my shirt and pranced around his body, getting him hot and me hotter. I didn't wear a bra. I bent forward and dropped my nipples in his mouth, "Now suck them." He raised his hand to touch them. "Don't touch them with anything but your mouth," I demanded. I went to my knees in front of him. "You're not sucking hard enough. Next time I'm going to spank you, do you hear me, Mr. Blackstone?"

"I want to be punished. I need to be punished," he confessed.

"Why?" I asked, curious for his answer.

"When I'm in love, I can't handle it. I have too many distractions, and I can't devote my attention to the woman I love." I listened, but he didn't go further. "I need you now," he said, begging for release.

I stepped out of my skirt. I'd come prepared for him. I had on a black garter belt and no panties.

I took my stance in front of his face. "You can't have this," I said, pointing to my mound.

"I want it." He followed me around on his knees. "I want that hot cunt." I stepped back and rubbed my clit over his face. I stood over him, and he leaned into me, swirling his tongue, and sucking the rim of my clit. He was hungry like an animal. I wanted to scream. I wanted to hold him and tell him that I was Alex. The pleasure of his head in my pussy brought me to orgasm, and I released my sexual frustration and pleasure. His tongue lapped it up like a cat drinking milk.

Moving away from him, I took the end of his belt and led him around, then I reached in my desk to pull out a large black leather belt with spikes. Slowly I teased the belt across his hard tanned buttocks. I wondered where he got that tan, because San Francisco had been overcast for a week. Mexico or the islands was my guess. "Do you want a contract?" I asked him.

"Only if it is to keep you exclusively mine. I can give you whatever you want." He looked at me like a high-school boy trying to score a girlfriend."

*I want you, you handsome fucked-up man. Can't you see, it's me, Alex,* I thought, trying for mental telepathy. "I can't guarantee that I will be exclusive to you," I said, watching his face.

"I can't accept that answer. We'll discuss that later. You know what I want now. Give it to me."

I saw a chill of bumps stand on his body. I hit him with all my might, punishing him for leaving me, and punishing him for opening himself up to Rebecca, when I loved him with all my being.

He reached for me, his penis was even harder now with his punishment, and he pulled me to my knees facing him. "I want your beautiful ass."

"I can't give my ass to you just like that. You have to beg me for it."

I hadn't gotten this far into the BDSM manual. Was this part of the Bondage thing? It sounded inviting, but was I giving too much? *Would he respect me in the morning?* I questioned myself, and the answer came back, *This is not about respect. You wanted respect when you were a virgin, and he fucked you and left without returning or contacting you.* I answered my question.

"I want that sweet ass. I need it."

"Why do you need it?"

"I need all of you. It's so beautiful, you remind me..." His attention faded, and then his eyes focused on me on my knees with my back to him. Teasing him. Torturing him.

He grabbed my long blonde wig, pulling it as he leaned into my ass, sticking his face in and then his tongue. After he had his feast, with me in the same position, and his hands firmly clutching my hips, he stated, "I need all of you, because I never want you to leave me. I need this. I need you to be mine in every possible way." I had to ask myself if I wanted to continue. "Few people understand what it's like being me. I don't sleep until I'm exhausted."

Yes, I wanted to continue. I wanted to be with him.

I smiled and pushed my ass into his face. He lifted himself behind me, putting on latex. I felt his fingers rimming the opening to my vagina until he was satisfied, then he reached for his hard dick and slapped my butt with it, and with a slap I jumped, then he drove his dick into my opening.

The pain was excruciating, but pleasurable, and I gave a low moan at first, then a trail of moans, "Oh. Oh. Oh." I turned my head and Max was kissing my back as he rode me, thrusting his dick in and out of my vagina as he fingered my pussy.

"I know I should have taken it easy, but I had no idea that your pussy would be this good," he said, kissing my back as an apology. "I love you and that ass," he said, stroking it softly. Was this part of sadomasochism, or was he into it all?

I began to enjoy that beautiful man fucking me and confessing his sins.

*Whoa... this can't be, I'm the one that is being sucked in. I'm in to him too much*, I thought.

"I want you to come on my fingers, I'm going to take my dick out, I'm not ready, and I want to enter your hot ass." I can't resist any part of you. I want all of you. And then I'm going to drop my load in your ass." His appetite covered more than BDSM.

His dirty talk heightened my arousal. He explained everything, but when he thrust it in, my ass was tight and I could feel him move inch by inch, until it felt as if his dick had reached my throat. The pain was heightened and the pleasure unbelievable. When he drove in further, I released liquid on his fingers. He placed his fingers to his mouth, and said, "I like your smell and the taste of you, it's intoxicating."

He kept pumping my ass over and over, until he groaned with pleasure, saying, "I'm emptying all my life into your beautiful ass. You will not leave me. Promise me." His voice became deep and dark, "Say it."

"I won't go until you tell me." I had given in to him. He was the Dom now, and I was now the sub. I had not planned for that. *He is good.*

Once again, I was where I had dreamed of—in his arms, but only for a minute. A small knock and my secretary's voice was heard, saying, "Mr. Blackstone, Mr. Blackstone, you have to get ready for your hotel's opening. It's ten o'clock."

We had been at it for two hours. I bet he would sleep well tonight.

"Do you want to come with me?" he said. "I hate those things; I just want to spend the day lying in bed with you, enjoying you. I want to get to know you."

"We need a contract," I said. "We need to determine who the Dom and who is the sub."

He looked at me long and pensive. "Why can't we come to an agreement now? Can't we reverse roles?"

"I'll think about it. Now you have to go to your opening." I helped him with his clothes. He gazed into my eyes, turned his head to the side, and a soft smile dashed across his face. "I'll see you later." He unlocked the door to his office and left, then I heard his shower.

After he'd gone out of the door, I hid behind it, then ran to my restroom. *What a perk, now I know why my office has a shower and a fancy toilet.* I took a long shower and sat on the bench, letting the hot water caress my legs, standing and turning my ass in the direction of the shower head to calm my anus. I could feel every thrust that Max had made. I had to admit that I had enjoyed every inch of his hard dick, every inch of his beautiful hard body, and every inch of his hard thrusts. I had to admit that I enjoyed him in every way. He had introduced me to a different life, but did I want to venture that far?

I'd intruded into his life for revenge, and now I was enjoying being with him, even if I had to accept his lifestyle. I walked out of the shower in a quandary, turned the small flat screen on to the local news. There was my Mr. Black being interviewed about Blackstone Millennium Hotel Chains. The date was a week ago. The reporter asked about his engagement. *Oh shit!* Anger could not describe how I felt. I'd just spent two hours giving everything to this man, and he was planning on marrying some rich virgin.

"Well, I'll see about that."

He said he didn't discuss his private life, and then flashed those perfect teeth with a tan that made me hot, but I couldn't get past my jealousy. *To become a Dom and sub I have to be aloof, and leave my feelings out of it,* I thought. But how could I? "I can't do this," I said.

I got back to work, but I couldn't concentrate. I couldn't wait until four o'clock came. I packed my things and rushed out of the building, and headed for the apartment. When I walked in, the doorman greeted me with a smile, and, "Nice weather we're having, Ms. Johns." How did he know my name? I stepped back, and asked, "I didn't know you were aware of my name."

"Yes, Ms. Johns. You have the penthouse apartment." He showed me my picture and name on his computer. Shaking with anger, I headed for Joshua's apartment, and found him with his head buried in his iPad. He heard my footsteps and turned, looking at me.

"Just leave the key in the Chinese bowl, then pick up your key, and take a tour of your new apartment."

"What? What is going on?" I questioned.

"You tell me. A group of Blackstone's people came over and moved your things into the penthouse."

"Wait a minute, you let them do that?"

"What was I to do Alex? This apartment belongs to Blackstone. I don't have enough money to afford this, and to tell you the truth, I like this apartment, and I like this job. So, take your high-maintenance ass over there, and let's see how the other half lives."

We left the apartment to do a tour of the penthouse. "Oh, my goodness, I can't accept this." The room was decorated with ultra-modern furniture, and the walls were covered with abstract and old masters. I recognized a painting by Miro, priceless. The bedroom was the largest I had ever seen, and it contained a California King. This brought back old memories of Montana.

I opened the closet, and rows of suits, shirts, gowns, dresses, and shoes. I was like a child in a candy store—touching everything. Joshua explored the other rooms, and found himself in the kitchen.

In the bedroom, I hit a button trying to open the drapes, and turned on the lights and a hidden door opened. "What is this?" Cautiously I stumbled into the dark room, and found the light switch. I stood with my mouth ajar. Ropes, leather undergarments, a mask. I picked up the ropes. "What the hell am I going to do with this?"

I heard Joshua coming into the bedroom, and I rushed out of the room to cut him off. "Do you believe this? There is only yogurt, nuts, and water. Does he expect you to live on this shit?" he said, holding up a bottle of imported water, opening it, and drinking it in one gulp. Leaning into the closet, he exclaimed, "Holy shit, you hit it big."

"I wouldn't call it that."

"What would you call it?"

"Control. That controlling fuck wants to have his cake and eat it too. I'm going to make his life miserable, until he doesn't know what or who he wants."

"Don't make it too miserable, you know I'm in this with you," Joshua said, reminding me that there was more at stake than my revenge.

We ordered in, Chinese food, General Tso's chicken and steamed vegetables for me, and shrimp with lobster sauce. It was the best Chinese food, even by New York's standards.

I sent Joshua home happy, because the meal was on me.

After a long day of fucking Mr. Black and eating Chinese, I climbed into that huge bed alone. I promptly fell asleep, until my work iPhone rang. It was on the table near the bed, and I fumbled around trying to find it and pressed the on button.

"Rebecca, I need to see you."

"What time is it? And who is this?"

"This is your Dom." I sat up and looked at the time on my phone. It was 2 a.m.

"Max, what do you want? I have to work tomorrow," I said groggily, clearing my eyes with my hand.

"You know what I want. I can't sleep and you don't have to work if you don't want to. I'm coming up. I have something for you."

"No... Don't..." He had already cut me off. I rushed to the bathroom and combed my blonde wig, stuffing my dark hair underneath it. I pinned it under the wig, hoping that my dark hair would not peek through. He knew by now that I wasn't a natural blonde, but once I took off that wig and the eyelashes, he would soon remember who I was. I wasn't ready for any disclosures before I had extracted my revenge on his perfectly formed ass.

# Chapter 6

Hearing the sound of a key opening the door, I glanced in that direction. Staring at me with sexy green eyes, long legs spread, and feet planted firmly, stood Max.

I felt my breath hitch. "Mr. Blackstone, what can I do for you this time of night?" Moving closer to me, untying the belt on his light beige trench coat, over his traditional dark silk V-neck sweater hugging his shoulders, caressing his beautiful chest, his dark slacks massaging his firm ass, loafers to match his pants, he wore a disarming smile, and a twinkle in his eye.

I concluded that he wanted me as much as I desired him. Max reached into his pocket and held out a folded piece of paper.

"What is it?"

"A contract."

"I told you several times that I couldn't be yours exclusively." He took a step in my direction, and I gazed into his eyes. Our eyes locked. His look disarmed me, and signaled that he had me, and that I would do anything for him. Max's body language signaled that he was far away, focused on something or someone. Maybe that was why he couldn't sleep. Although I represented something that he enjoyed, I was just a piece of property, something he could acquire as he had done everything else in his life, something he could dominate and oversee, like his companies.

Reaching for the contract, I threw it down on the sofa, never looking at it, or where it landed. I wanted him badly. I could feel it with my throbbing clit.

"It's late and I'm not in the mood." I turned on my heels, but he grabbed my arm, stopping me in my tracks.

His tone was dark, "Let me put you in the mood," he said, eyes flaming.

"Mr...."

"Call me Max. Call me anything but Mister. We've been more intimate than a man and wife."

"I saw the news and a reporter asked about your fiancée." I peered into his eyes, then down to those firm pecs and large hands.

"That's what you're breaking my balls over? I'm yours, can't you tell when a man is hot for you." He reached for me, and I moved away. "I want you to be the Dom." He swallowed hard. "I'm willing to do anything for you. I only felt this way once before in my life. I can recognize that I need you, and I'm willing to give in to you. Maybe we can agree on a power exchange, where we switch. That was the purpose of the contract, and giving me exclusive rights over you."

*Yeah, he's good. He knows how to compromise until he gets what he wants,* I thought. "You haven't answered my question about your fiancée," I said, meeting his soft gaze.

"That was nothing; I broke that engagement three years ago, because I had met a girl, but she left me and I never saw her again. It's over. You have me exclusively," he said, taking off his coat and dropping it on the chair.

"Can we discuss the apartment and clothes?"

"No, it's in the initial contract."

*The one I never bothered to read.* He eased his face close, smelling me then kissing my neck. "I want to discuss that room with the ropes," I said, breaking the embrace.

"It's in the contract," he said, nibbling on my ear, pulling the straps on my silk gown with his teeth, and dropping it to the floor, until I was naked. He grabbed my breasts in his hands, shoved my nipple in his mouth, and sucked it painfully hard, until it peaked and was a bright red. He moved his tongue around it until it stood hard, and he began working on the next breast with both hands and tongue. He stepped back, looking at me gasping for breath, his gaze penetrating my skin.

"I need to shower," I admitted.

"I don't want you to. I want to smell you; your natural smell makes me hard. See, and he looked down and my eyes followed. I reached over and unzipped his pants, unhooked the top, and they fell at his feet. He stepped out of his pants barefoot and without underwear. He pulled the sweater over his head and dropped it on a chair. Both he and I were staring each other down, waiting for who would be the Dom and who would be the sub.

"Suck my dick, "he commanded, and I went to my knees before I had time to protest. "See, that wasn't so hard," he said, clutching my shoulders with his strong hands. It appeared so natural. He stood straight as if commanding soldiers in the army.

*I have not signed up for this,* I thought, but I enjoyed placing his hard dick in my mouth and watching his handsome face. I knew from my first lesson what Max wanted. Taking his penis in my hand, rimming the head around my heated lips, I watched his face show his pleasure. He guided it, occasionally pulling it out, then shoving it as far inside my mouth as I could take it.

His gorgeous body stood with his chest forward, heaving up and down, his head leaning back, and his eyes closed. I had him lost in ecstasy. I suddenly realized that I was in control, and although I was performing the acts that he enjoyed and commanded me, he controlled nothing. I felt free to enjoy myself with the love of my life, The Incredible Mr. Black.

Max pulled his dick from my mouth just as my pussy was wet and weeping for more. I wanted to suck him off. He leaned over me and brought me to lie on his twenty-thousand-dollar rug. He lay across and then I rolled over and sat on top of him, rubbing my breasts across his mouth. He had a strange look on his face. "You remind me of someone, that's why I'm so drawn to you."

"Was she a Dom or a sub?"

"She was vanilla." His gaze lingered outward. "Now is not the time to discuss her."

"Well then, we need to address the ropes and handcuffs."

"What is there to discuss?"

"I don't think I can play your games. I want more."

"What do you want? Just ask. I'll give it to you. He stated breathlessly. Do you want a car; I'll send you one tomorrow. I'll buy you a house wherever you want."

"I don't want things. They mean nothing to me."

"Then, what do you want?" he said, voice quivering.

"I want your heart."

Silence cut the air like a sharp knife cutting paper. He rolled me over, so now he was looking down on me, assuming the active role.

"I can't give you my heart now. All I know now is that I need your body. My heart..." he rambled, and I cut off his statement. I interrupted him, because I didn't want him to finish.

He climbed off of me and walked over to lie in the bed. I sat on the floor with my back leaning on the bed.

"I guess I asked for that," I admitted. Pain coursed from my head to my feet, but I pretended that I wasn't affected."

I had agreed to this exciting, illicit, sordid, tempting, sexual eroticism. I had accepted him on his terms, because I loved him so much.

When Max didn't respond, I glanced up. He had fallen asleep. I covered him up and climbed in crawling next to him under the silk covers. Sleep didn't come easy, and before I could close my eyes, his long fingers were massaging my clit, making it wet.

"You have kept me up the entire night, how am I going to get to work?"

"Work from home. I want to continue what we started."

"You barely slept," I said.

Standing and then opening the closet, Max revealed a world into itself, a BDSM room. The room had a padded table, bench, and small bed, with various types of ropes hanging on the wall. I spotted the dildo that Max had referred to in his text.

He passed his hands on instruments of punishment, taking time to glare at me with a dark smirk, raising his brow when touching an anal kit, containing lubes, beads, and a probe.

Picking out handcuffs, he held them in front of me. "Don't worry, they're not for you. Put them on me." Closing the door to the large closet, he lay his hard naked body on the small bed, with his hands in front of him.

I hitched his arms one at a time, cuffing first the right wrist, then the left to the headboard designed specifically for handcuffs. His gaze never wavered, his eyes were on my bare breasts. He slid his tongue across his lips.

As I clasped the second handcuff, I saw his cock rise. "Now I command you to suck me until you feel me dripping, but don't make me come. If you do, then I'm going to spank you each time you allow it to happen. Take off that thong, and put on those high heels lying near the bed."

"Yes, Master." I surprised myself. I didn't know where that came from. I found that I enjoyed the games, and I wanted to be a part of it, because I wanted to be with the incredible Mr. Black.

I shoved his hard penis into my mouth, and I leaned over him balancing on my hands. I reached for his nicely shaped dick, which fitted in my hand, mouth, and pussy. "No, use only your mouth, not your hand." Up and down, I sucked and moved my tongue to rim and lick the head of his penis. I spied his head lift and fall back, his mouth wide and his breathing intense. I tasted his sweet liquid, and I knew that his cream would burst into my mouth. I wanted it, but he had commanded me not to bring him to orgasm. I peered up at his strong handsome face, and my pussy leaked with come at his pleasure.

Carried away with pleasing him, I forgot about his command, and I wanted to experience his spanking. His gazed settled on me. "You have forced me to come, sub. I directed you not to do that, you have disobeyed me, and you know what that means." I wiped my mouth and swallowed his sweet cum. "I'll have to spank you. Now release me and get my belt."

"I want you..." I said, when Max interrupted.

"You are not supposed to speak to me unless I require it. Now get the belt." I gave him a defiant gaze. "If we are to be together, then you have to learn how to be a sub. I own clubs that can help you learn about my lifestyle, because it's apparent that you need lessons. And I will start by spanking you now. Lie across that table on your stomach."

The next day my behind was sore and bruised. After Max spanked my ass, he kissed it all over and then rubbed it with ointment to ease the healing. His eyes demonstrated that his heart wasn't into hurting me, but I had begun to enjoy the pain, which brought exhilaration and pleasure all over. We were caught up in the moment, and I let it go too far. He asked for a safe word, but I didn't give it. My pain threshold was high. The next morning, he kissed me and my behind, and left for work. He had another apartment in San Francisco where he lived another life away from BDSM. He never discussed it with me or brought me there. He was deep into the BDSM life, and he wanted me with him.

I didn't know how long I could follow him. I wanted more from him, I wanted him. Now I would be forced to bring Alex out of hiding if I was to have a chance with Max. It was time to put Rebecca aside, and allow Alex to take over.

I scrambled to find his business card, searching through my ridiculously priced designer bag, "Ah there it is." My private iPhone said 9 a.m. "That's a great time. I know Max's schedule. He's probably in his limousine on his way to a meeting."

The phone rang, and Max answered, "Hello."

"Mr. Blackstone... you previously handed me your card, and stated that you would wait for my call. Well, this is my call."

"I'm sorry, but can you refresh my memory?"

"I was sitting in a pub with a man, and you walked to my table and said that I reminded you of someone. You noted that I was not married, and that you wanted to see me."

"Yes... yes, I remember." His voice was light and excited, showing signs of nervousness, which made me more confident. "Will you have dinner with me?"

"I'm not sure if I have time tonight."

"You can make time, because I will make time for you. I'll have my limo driver pick you up at eight."

"No, I prefer to meet you at the restaurant."

"Very well, I'll have my secretary contact you. You can provide her all the necessary information, including your name. I'm sorry but I have another call."

# Chapter 7

E xcited to be myself again, I bought with my own money, a lovely clinging red dress I was dying to wear to meet the man I loved, not as Rebecca, but as Alex. I paired it with black pumps and a black belt. I called Joshua, and he agreed to take me in his company car to San Francisco's downtown area.

The restaurant was located in one of Blackstone's hotels, *How convenient!*

"Alex, you look gorgeous," Joshua said, taking my hand, turning me in circles and peering at me like a potential pervert, and by the way he surveyed my ass, he probably had a fetish working somewhere.

"You're just saying that, Joshua, because you want to get into my panties."

"Not so. Well, maybe. I just love you for yourself, and because you've been a friend."

"Oh, how sweet." I gave him a kiss on his cheek.

He stopped in front of a glass building with LED lighting beaming Blackstone Omni Hotel. *Impressive.* The first thing crossing my mind—*Max never brought Rebecca here. Maybe he's ashamed of Rebecca. Maybe he wants to keep that life with her a secret. If that's the case, I will never have that man, especially if I keep up this charade. Wasn't the main idea to exact revenge?* I asked myself. Now I was becoming ambitious. I was thinking of having him to myself. *As Rebecca or Alex?* I questioned. *Does it matter?* I couldn't answer that now, because I didn't know the answer.

All my thoughts were ghosts that haunted me as I sashayed into the hotel, not knowing what to expect. I entered the restaurant, and a young woman dressed in a black suit led me into a private room with large booths and tables.

"Mr. Blackstone will be here shortly, will you have a booth or table?"

"A booth would be nice." She held out her hand, and I sat in a small private booth.

"Can I bring you a drink?"

"No thank you, not at this time."

No sooner had I sat, when in walked my Mr. Black. He strutted in wearing a dark suit and white shirt, and lately hair on his face that made him look incredible, and sensuous. It appeared he had taken off his tie and was ready to relax. "Alex."

I was shocked that he remembered my name. "You remember me."

"I will never forget you, Ms. Bishop," he murmured.

"Where did you go, and why did you take yourself from me, when I loved you from the time I met you? I still think of you and now you're here. It is fortuitous." He sat close to me and reached for my hand, peering into my eyes, searching for something and then kissed my hand. "Why are you looking at me like that?" I said, with a crack in my voice, and trying to still my trembling hands.

"You look beautiful in that color, it's exciting and seductive. You remind me of someone, but she's nothing like you. You know that you have stolen my heart and made me a wreck for years. How long has it been?"

"Three years," *you beautiful fuck. Three years I have been suffering. For three years I have wanted to hear you tell me that you love me,* my thoughts shouted.

"What have you been doing in that time?"

*Having your baby, fucking you, and loving you,* my thoughts interrupted.

"And what are you doing here?"

*Getting my revenge, you beautiful, sexy, intriguing man.* "I enrolled in graduate school, then dropped out when I found a position at a hospital in the Bay area."

"Why don't you work for me at one of my hotels? I hired a friend of yours from Montana

"Yes. I know. I ran into Joshua in a restaurant one day." I paused, searching his eyes. "I was your employee once, and it didn't work out..."

"Because, you disappeared before I could..."

"Call me and explain why after you fucked me you never called."

"Yes, but you had resigned. I put resources to find you, but you dropped off the grid." After clearing the air, we laughed, we ordered food, and we drank a lot of wine. "I want you to know where I live when I'm in San Francisco," he said.

I felt lucky that he wanted to show Alex his home and not Rebecca. He took my hand, his staff and guests looked on in awe and envy as we strolled hand in hand to a private elevator. Putting in the key, he never released my hand. The elevator headed straight up to the Presidential Suite. His eyes never left me. He was a perfect gentleman, not the hot horny fuck I had just left, who can't keep his hands off my pussy, and his dick out of my ass.

He was as much a chameleon as I was. He was a different man with Alex to how he was with Rebecca. With Alex he was soft and vulnerable, but with Rebecca he was tough and domineering. He had a dual personality. That was probably why he needed two women. I was his one woman with a dual persona. We were made for each other.

The suite with exquisite contemporary furnishings and abstract paintings housed three large bedrooms and baths, with killer views of San Francisco Bay and the Golden Gate Bridge. One bedroom belonged to his butler, and the largest was where he slept, when he could sleep, which wasn't much. I suddenly became nervous. I didn't want to repeat the last mistake I made with him. He still didn't discuss Rebecca, so I decided to bring up the subject.

"Do you have a special someone waiting for the Incredible Mr. Blackstone?" I questioned, and searched eyes.

"No one you have to worry about." He sounded so definite that I thought maybe I should worry.

"Mr. Blackstone..."

"Call me Max... I want to marry you," he blurted out.

"Marry me? You have seen me only twice in your life," I said in shock.

"I feel that we have never been apart from each other."

*We haven't been apart, you sensuous fuck, love of my life, man of my dreams. Your dick has been in my mouth, and your gorgeous face and body have been in my dreams from the moment I met you.*

"Before I answer you, you need to get rid of your attachments. And we have plenty to discuss. If by tomorrow you still want to marry me, call me. Here's my card. I dropped the newly minted card on the table. I should be going," I said coldly.

He watched me, surprised, not knowing what to say, then tilting his head, "I'll see you out, and my driver will take you home."

"No, I can manage; I haven't given you my answer yet. For now, I'm an independent woman, and I need time to think about you and your offer."

He held me around the waist, to ask one more question, "I was the first. Has another man tasted that sweet pussy, and gotten close to that sweet ass?"

Turning to face him, I replied, "You know everything about me; don't you know whether I have had other men? You knew I was a virgin. Don't you know who I'm sleeping with now, or are you too preoccupied to bother?" I gave him a wink and a sweet smile.

He followed me. "You're exasperating. I wish I could put you over my knee and spank you."

"You may get a chance yet." That was a promise I knew he couldn't resist. My mind wandered: *Are you blind? You have spanked my ass, you handsome fuck. I know what you really want, a vanilla, and you want Rebecca. You want it all, Mr. Black. You want to use your ropes and whips, leathers, handcuffs, and anal beads on me, but you don't know how to introduce it for fear I will not accept you. It would be easier to marry Rebecca, but that's not what you really want. You want your deflowered virgin too. What are you doing, Mr. Black?*

# Chapter 8

O n a clear Sunday morning, I pulled out my diary, which was hidden in the back of my closet behind a row of crippling expensive high-heeled shoes, I would never wear outside of this apartment; it was time to document this.

Sunday, March 1

By this time, I have Max completely confused. He doesn't know which woman he wants, Alex the vanilla, or Rebecca his uncontrollable slutty Dom and sometimes sub. I enjoyed the events unfolding each day, until I realized that he would see me as deceptive and manipulative. He chose me because he loved and trusted me. He wanted Rebecca, because he needed her to cope with his world of stress. How am I to break the news to him without destroying his trust and perhaps having him walk away from both? But then, that is the least of my worries.

Monday, March 2

Max is hiding a secret of his own, and it is not just his relationship with Rebecca. He has professed his love for me, yet he is continuing his midnight sexual romps with Rebecca, which has me exhausted and ready to call an end to it. He hasn't said a word about his life of BDSM, even though he asked me to marry him. I conclude that he's planning to continue his erotic life and I'm becoming more entrenched in that lifestyle every minute I spend with him as Rebecca.

Tuesday, March 3

Lately Max has resorted to calling Alex late at night for dirty talk, then he shows up at Rebecca's place to relieve the tension that's been smoldering during the day. I haven't seen him at work, but he's prompt in the middle of the night to get his sexual fix. I wonder what he's up to now. As soon as these thoughts left my mind the phone rang. I'm having trouble keeping my identities in order. I can't keep this up much longer, too much time spent as Rebecca when it's obvious that Max wants to keep that life a secret. This has to end soon.

"Hello," I said with a low soft moan.

"Alex, you are turning me on. How long are you going to deny me your body?"

"Until we're married," I said with a silent laugh.

"You're going to kill me, baby."

*The only thing that's going to kill you is all that fucking,* I thought.

"Alex, do you have an iPad?"

*Now what does he want now. I've concluded that my Mr. Black is a sex addict.* "Yes, why? I'm in bed, Max." *I hope he doesn't ask to come to Alex's apartment. I've had to rent a room just to have an address in case he has someone watching me, or he wants to pick me up for a date.*

"Can I see you now?"

"No," I said, raising my voice. I have to be in work early."

"Turn on the iPad. I want to see your face and body."

*Oh, that's what you want, you horny handsome sex addict.* I did as he said to keep him away from my small room across town. Now he can go to Rebecca's apartment. "Put your breasts close to the camera, now move the iPad down to my pussy. It's mine isn't it?" he questioned.

"I'm sure by now you know the answer to that question." *He thinks he has two women and two vaginas to crawl into. I can only imagine what he'll say when he discovers that his acquisition is somewhat smaller than he thinks.*

I heard his breathing, and he said that he had to go and would call tomorrow. It was less than an hour when Mr. Black entered my penthouse apartment with a hard dick.

"I haven't seen you, where have you been, Max?" *I wish I could laugh out loud.*

"Does it matter, Rebecca? We're together now," he said in a disinterested murmur.

"I explained Max, that I need more from you."

"And I said I can't give you what you want." His gaze fell on my diary. I took his hands leading him to the door.

"Then you will have to leave."

I saw the panic in his eyes. "I can't leave, I need you."

"Show me how much you need me." He stripped his clothes from that sexy body, crawled on all fours, then passing his gaze upward, begged me to whip him, and I gladly did as he requested.

"Why am I whipping you?" I asked, trailing the leather strap across his back, then giving him a hard whack across his buttocks.

"Because I have been..." but he wouldn't confess that he was going to marry Alex. "I want to eat you," he confessed.

"Beg me." *Admit you want me, you beautiful sexy fuck.*

"I need to smell you. Let me put my face in your cunt." I stood over him as he sat on his expensive rug and he bent his head back, sticking his tongue in my clit as he held my butt with both hands. Looking up at me, he admitted, "I can't do without you."

"Why don't you admit that you love me?"

"I do love you, but I'm going to marry someone else, because I love her too." *I tried to remain dispassionate and calm, and remember that I was both women, and that it didn't make sense to be jealous of myself.* My expression eased and my brow smoothed.

"Why are you with me? Why aren't you with her?"

"She can't satisfy me the way you can. My problem is that you want to dominate me, and I want you too, but I need a submissive."

"So, she is a sub, and that's why you're marrying her."

"No, she's vanilla."

"And that's what you want?"

"No, I want both."

"You can't have both," I said, having a good laugh at Max's expense. This was the moment I lived for—to see him frustrated and confused. I continued with the charade to see where and when it would end.

"Rebecca, if we are to continue our relationship, you will have to learn to be a sub. I have made plans for you to attend a retreat to master the art of bondage. If we are to continue our relationship, there is more you need to learn about my world."

*This is not what I've planned for.* I thought. *I'll never be able to carry this out. Maybe I should confess and kick him out, but I can't, I'm afraid of losing my beautiful man.*

Max suggested that I needed extensive training, because I was getting out of hand. I didn't listen to his commands and was too dominant. He just wanted time to spend with Alex,

*Oh, he will get a surprise when Alex tells him she will be in Seattle.*

After an exhausting night, I woke turning over to see the left side of the bed empty, and a note carefully placed on his pillow.

Rebecca,

I have a meeting, and later I have a flight to Colorado for a conference. I will be occupied for two days. I've made arrangements for you to attend Pandora's Retreat. You will discover that it is what you need to ensure that we are on the same page, and that your experience there will bring a fresh approach to our relationship.

Max

I couldn't figure out what I hated most, those stupid notes, or his refusal to tell Rebecca that he loved her.

After a long day at work, and now dealing with Max at night, trying to keep track of my phones and my voice as Rebecca, I knew this would end badly. My private phone rang.

"Alex, I have a week off, can we get together to discuss our engagement and wedding?"

"Oh, hello Max, I'm sorry, but I have to see my parents in Seattle."

"I can send my jet and take you, and I can meet your parents."

"No... no... I think I should tell them myself. I'm their only daughter and I know they will ask me all sorts of questions. I'll have you meet them later."

"I miss you. Don't go away from me."

"The way you left me."

"That was cruel, Alex."

"I apologize, Max. I never want to hurt you."

"Is there anything you need to tell me, Alex?"

*Yes, I love you so much, and I have a confession to make. But you'll never hear it now, my handsome beautiful Mr. Black.* "When you return, I'll tell you everything Max, we need to be truthful with each other if we are going to have a life together." *I am trying to give him a way out. Give him an opportunity to tell me about Rebecca.*

"Can you meet me at my apartment tomorrow, before you leave?" he said with a low melancholy voice.

"Okay, but I can't stay long."

I rushed home from work, showered, and dressed, asked Josh to drop me off at Max's apartment. We drove in silence; Josh saw a tired body, tired from my dual role of dealings with Max.

"When are you going to tell him that you are Rebecca, Alex?"

"I can't tell him now. I'm going to do it soon. I can't take this anymore, I'm exhausted."

"He parked and glanced my way." I don't know how to tell you this, but he has been married."

"He's a good-looking man in his thirties, I'm not surprise." But oh was I! I tried not to show my feelings even though I was beyond pissed.

"Well, since you aren't affected by this, then maybe you should know that he has been married three times and divorced before he's thirty. Do you want to become his fourth wife?"

I jumped out of the car and didn't say a word, rushing through the door, lumbering to the front desk asking for Mr. Blackstone. The young man pointed to the elevator and a security guard unlocked it. I marched in, and it stopped at the penthouse. I stepped into the beautiful apartment, with the beautiful man standing waiting for me.

"I had dinner brought up." Reaching for my hands he led me to the terrace. "Is this okay?" he said uncovering the main course.

"Wonderful."

Max lifted his gaze behind me and across the Bay and I knew he was thinking of Rebecca.

We ate, danced, and when I thought he wanted to fuck, I said, "My flight is early in the morning, I can't stay."

He insisted that his jet fly me there. I refused again, then he opened a small box, and went to his knees. "Will you marry me, Alex?" My mind was in a whirl, "Alex, Alex, Alex, what's wrong?"

"Nothing." I forgot that I was Alex. I was so hot for him and so angry with him, but I couldn't make love to him, because he would know everything, and my plan would be shot to hell. I managed to pull myself away, telling Max that a cab was waiting. Visually angry, a raised eyebrow, that he couldn't do something for me, not even have his driver take me home, he stood waiting for an answer.

"Yes, I'll marry you." *Have you lost your mind, Alex? You don't know this man.*

It was the largest yellow-diamond engagement ring I had ever seen. In fact, it was the first yellow diamond I had ever seen. I took control of my emotions, I wanted to say: *Oh my God,* and kiss his manicured hand. I wanted to say: *Fuck me any which way you can,* but I didn't. I wanted to give him a blow job, but I didn't. He placed that rock on my finger and I let him. Smiling inside, I strutted full of confidence to the elevator with him holding on to my hand for dear life.

To his surprise I put my hand on his cock, and gave him a massage reminiscent of Rebecca, and he agreed to a long engagement to get to know each other, then I left him, feeling used, not knowing whether he would see me again.

He didn't know who I had become and where I lived. I could disappear and never have to see his rich, sexy, hard to get out of my mind, thrice-married fuck, again. But who was I kidding? I fell deeper and deeper in love with him. But I wanted to know why he had been married three times and divorced them all.

I refused the idea of the ropes without trying them. He declared that he couldn't tolerate my behavior. And because of that he was sending me off for a lesson in discipline, like I was a child who disobeyed her parents. That was why I was walking through the doors of Pandora's Retreat, to learn what was expected of a sub.

Entering the room, I glanced around and there were tables, chairs, and instruments to cause pain and pleasure.

I had accepted Mr. Black's world. By sending me here, he was not planning on leaving Rebecca to be true to me. The Dom came through the door. Immediately I felt a connection between us. It was eerie. I didn't know why my heart raced, and I became eager anticipating sexual arousal by this gorgeous man. Was it his drop-dead body that made me hot, wet, and confused? Or that mask that concealed nothing, not even those green eyes. Now I wanted to experience what I had denied—an attraction to sadomasochism, kinky sex, and bondage. He walked like Max, and his body was the image of Max.

*It is Max,* I thought. *Oh, this is getting good. I'll go along with him and teach his beautiful possessive ass a lesson. He thinks that he can fool me with those leather pants. It just makes him hot and glamorous.*

❧

"MR. BLACKSTONE, THE company has done a complete background check on Ms. Johns and Ms. Bishop," the head of security stated, carrying his iPad. Max leaped from his chair and walked around his desk to view the information. "I can send the information to your computer."

"Yes, please, but I want to hear this now." Max glanced with a raised eyebrow, and clutching the end of his desk. "The abbreviated version. *Now,*" Max demanded.

The chief of security, dressed in his perfectly ironed black suit and white shirt and striped tie, began reading, "The two women are one and the same. Ms. Johns formally known as Ms. Bishop has been working as your assistant under the name Rebecca Johns." He paused to look up at Max's furrowed brow. "Ms. Bishop first worked for your company three years ago. After leaving, she returned to Brooklyn where she gave birth to a son nine months later, and..."

"Wait a minute. Did you say a child?"

"Yes, sir, a boy. I was just getting to that. She didn't identify the father, but sent her son to live with her parents in Seattle, Washington. She has several degrees, and..."

"Stop right there, I will read the rest later, because I have an appointment."

Max asked to be left alone. He found his chair behind his desk and sank into it. Turning and staring out of the floor-to-ceiling windows, he called his chauffeur, requesting his car be made ready and waiting. His heart skipped in his chest and the sound rang loud. He placed his hand to his chest, as if to push it back to silence it.

He rushed to put on his jacket. How could he allow this to happen? What was Alex thinking? "I'm a father," he shouted. How could he have put her through this? He smiled to think about how she had fooled him. Why didn't he know? Max went over the first time he had met Alex and Rebecca. He had been too busy with work, dealing with his brother and trying to juggle Rebecca and Alex to notice. But, wait, they did smell the same, he remembered. Was he too involved in his own deceptions, his own pleasures, his own problems, to even know that he had bedded the same woman?

What else had he overlooked? He never looked beyond the blonde wig and eyelashes.

"I'm going to spank her when I see her," he whispered as he headed for the elevators. When he reached the elevators his staff looked on curious, he turned, and shouted, "I'm a father, and I have a son." He stopped in his tracks. It was because of him that she was heading for Pandora's Retreat. He felt that he would be sorry if he didn't make it there in time. He had to stop Alex from meeting the Master.

"My Alex would never allow a stranger to touch her. She's so young, everything is a game to her," he murmured.

If he didn't make it in time, they would both regret their decisions. But he most of all, he could lose her. He truly loved Alex and Rebecca, one of the perks of marrying Alex. A slight smile crossed his lips.

He desired Alex, because she was what he needed to complete his life—a woman he was sexually attracted to, a woman who knew what she wanted and went after it. And she had his child. This was what he needed to make him happy, and diminish the stress that was running rampant through his life.

Max wanted Alex to himself, and so far no one had touched her but him, and she was the mother of his child. He knew that that world of BDSM was seductive, and once she became entrenched in it, she might seek out others that would provide what she needed, and he would have been responsible.

In a daze he didn't remember exiting his building and entering his black limo, or greeting his chauffer.

"Faster... I need you to drive faster," a terrified Max shouted. His driver knew that it was impossible to go faster, because of the traffic. He had to travel out of San Francisco and across the Bay Bridge into the Berkley Hills.

"I don't know why you can't pass that car," Max said, but the driver didn't hear him. "Why would Alex play such a dangerous game with me?" But Max was glad she had, because he got to know the real Alex.

Alex signed in and was taken to a large room. A man wearing nothing except for tight leather jeans and a black leather mask greeted her. His chest was impressive, and at a glance his body could double for Maximilian. Alex felt an immediate attraction to him, her breathing intensified, and she felt heat settle low in her clit.

She relaxed and displayed the most enticing worldly smile. He marched around her, "Your clothes are acceptable for now, but there needs to be more flesh showing. Take off your top. My cock needs to be aroused immediately. Alex hurried and loosened the leather top, which fell to the floor, and her full breasts felt the chill and heat in the room. Her nipples rose from arousal at seeing the man she thought was Max relaxed in tight leather jeans.

She had crossed over to Max's world and she wanted to please him, and perhaps have a good laugh when he revealed that he was the Master. How funny would that be?

"We will begin with the ropes. Lie on the table on your stomach." Alex hesitated. "Did you hear me?"

"Yes, Master, but..."

"You shouldn't question what I say. Because you are new to this, the first day I will take it slow with you. Maybe we should try something different. I will just tie your wrists and legs, and if you want to continue shake your head. You should think of a safe word, because tomorrow's sessions will be more intense."

"My safe word is Black."

"Good. Now we can begin."

Alex lay on the table. Somehow she felt relaxed. His voice was soothing, but commanding, which seduced her and sent chills to her clit. She would experience it all in this week, and she would be with the man she loved. *What could be better?* She thought. However, a feeling of exhilaration and trepidation took hold of her. But what could be wrong if the love of her life sanctioned it, and wanted to take her higher? She forgot that she was Rebecca, and Max would never expose Alex to this world. She became jealous of Alex.

"Now I will give you a series of commands that you will follow."

Alex lowered her eyelids and faced the wall, lying flat on her stomach. "Place your hands behind your back." Alex did as she was commanded. The Master tied her wrists and then moving down the length of the table, reached for her legs, stroking them softly up and down to her butt, and down again, and tied them. "You're doing great," he said, walking around her naked body surveying her ass. Trailing his finger from the nape of her neck, he moved it down to her split, his finger lingering on each buttock, then swirling it around the rim of her anus.

Chills rose on her skin.

"Now I'm going to continue with the ropes. I'm going to bind you where your breasts are exposed, and the ropes will make a figure eight. This is done because I want to experiment with your breasts, and I don't want you to be able to move," the Master said, licking his dry lips.

He strutted in his tight jeans, and pulled out two clamps from a drawer. "I will put these on your nipples, and if you have pain that you can't endure, then use your safe word." He walked to the side of the table, and gently cupped her left breast and placed the clamp on her nipple. Alex felt excitement course down her breasts and land on her clit. He placed his hand between her legs, then put his finger in her opening, and when he pulled it out, it was wet.

"You are a good student. I can tell you are enjoying being bound, and I see you can take a lot of pain. You are my best pupil," he said with his eyes sparkling. "I know you can handle whatever level I take you to," he said, smiling as he snapped the clamp on Alex's right nipple. Still, she did not cry out or give her safe word. He placed his finger in her clit, and felt a vibration and he knew she was coming.

"You naughty girl, you are coming, and I didn't command you. I think I should punish you."

Confident that his pupil would make a good sub, he brought out a leather whip. He wanted to test her level of pain. Trailing it from her back and then striking her butt, *whack, whack, whack,* and still she didn't cry out. "How do you feel?"

"I can take more, Master."

"Can you take this?" He shoved a butt plug up her ass and still she never winced.

"Do you know what Top means?"

"Yes, Master. You are taking the active role."

"And you are...?"

"The bottom," Alex stated.

"Precisely. And if you are a good girl I will allow you to switch. You can be the Dom and I will be the sub tomorrow at our next session."

Alex found that she became more attracted to the man she thought was Max. There was something about him. She had never seen him relaxed before. He was carefree and fun.

She had become attracted to the handsome man under the mask with his curly dark hair, green eyes, and all six feet two of maleness.

His voice was smooth and seductive, when he spoke, she wanted to lie on that padded table, and let him have his way with her again and again.

"I know this is irregular, but I'm attracted to you more than I care to admit. I would like to penetrate your ass. That's my weakness. That's my fetish. It's something about you that I feel that I have to have it."

"You are the Master," Alex stated, wanting him to breach her ass as much as he wanted it.

"I'm going to take the plug out and then if you have discomfort use your safe word." He untied the ropes as quickly as he had bound her with them.

The Master said, "Get on all fours. I want to look on you for a few minutes." He stood breathing hard. Alex heard him inhale and exhale.

Alex took a deep breath. "Master, I'm having second thoughts," she said, still on all fours and completely naked except for the leather studded necklace she had placed around her neck for a fashion statement. She thought it would make her appear more knowledgeable about BDSM.

"I understand your apprehension," Master stated in a cool soothing voice. "Maybe I was too rough on you," he said, rubbing her ass with his strong hands. He stroked her butt, kissed it, calming her, seducing her, and when she lifted her butt, he grabbed his hard penis. Holding it, he place latex over his large member, as he took a second look at her inviting ass and prepared to mount her...

The door burst open, "Stop it, Jonas. Don't go any further," Maximilian shouted. Alex surprised and confused reached for a robe.

"What's the meaning of this? No one is allowed in here when I'm working," Jonas questioned Max.

"You were doing more than working. You were not to enter her anus or her vagina."

"He did not enter me, Max."

"I know my brother, and if I had not arrived in time he would have had you."

"Your brother?" Alex questioned, her voice reaching a crescendo. "How dare you allow your brother to...?"

"And are you Alex or Rebecca?"

"This is the woman you almost lost your mind over after she ran away from you?" Jonas Blackstone said laughing hysterically, while hitting Max on his back. I guess the laugh is on you, big brother."

"Come on, Alex, we are leaving now. I'm not letting you out of my sight." Max hitched his hand under Alex's arm and led her down the corridor. Jonas peeped out of the room and yelled, "Am I invited to the wedding?" Max didn't turn around, but just flipped Jonas the finger behind his back.

"Max, I will never forgive you for this." Alex headed in the direction of the small apartment.

"Don't worry about your clothes, take the robe and leave your car, someone will drive it to our apartment, and we're getting married. You're mine." He glanced at her, waiting for her answer.

"Yes, Master, but I want to be courted first."

"You're going to have to teach me."

"Do you mean that you never courted a woman?"

"Never."

"Do you have something to tell me, Alex?"

"I think you already know by the way you are looking at me. You know everything now about me. Our child..."

"Tell me everything about my son, then we are going into our room, and I'm going to spank that lovely ass," he said, arching his eyebrow.

"Max, do you have something to tell me?"

He stopped and peered at her with dark hooded eyes. "I have a confession to make and there are some things you need to know."

"Do you mean there is more besides you having a twin?"

"Not exactly what you think. I hope you will still want to marry me."

Alex felt that she knew what she needed, and that Max loved her even after the deception. "After you reveal your deep dark secrets, then you're going to wear this collar, and I'm going to put on my leather bikini and take out that whip." She paused, glancing at him. "You will sleep for a week," she said, letting out a laugh.

Stepping into the limo, Alex unzipped Max's pants, then looking up at Max. He hit a button, and the partition rose, cutting them off from the world.

Their gazes locked, she leaned forward, and he caressed her hair as she rolled his dick around the rim of her mouth. Max leaned his head forward, and stated, "That's why I love you. You are spontaneous and you know what I need."

"I want you to try to forget everything and everybody," Alex said, stroking the head of his dick. Max's head feathered back, and he closed his eyes, and her mouth curled around his hard aroused penis. She felt his pulse of life vibrate in her mouth. Her head bobbed up and down on his hard cock, and she stole a look at his beautiful face. Peace had settled in to the small lines etched near his eyes. Alex's gaze got lost on his face, wandered down and settled on the evening paper. She didn't know why it caught her gaze, maybe it was the headlines:

*Fiancée of Notorious Billionaire Industrialist Maximilian Blackstone found Strangled.*

The End

## Book 2 Temptation in Black Next

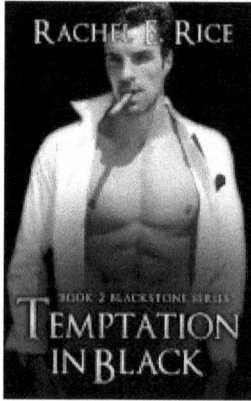

There are more books in this series.

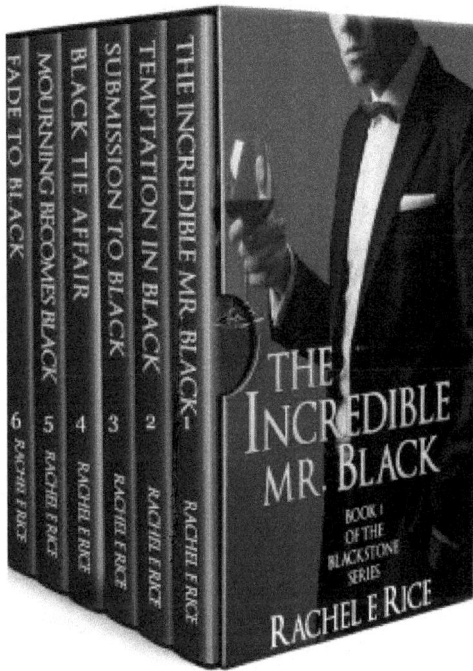

Thank you for reading my books. Please leave a review if you enjoyed them. Below you will find a list of my books. Leave a message at rachelerice04@gmail.com or visit my website for excerpts from my books at: www.rachel-e-rice.com

BLACKOUT Coming in 2023

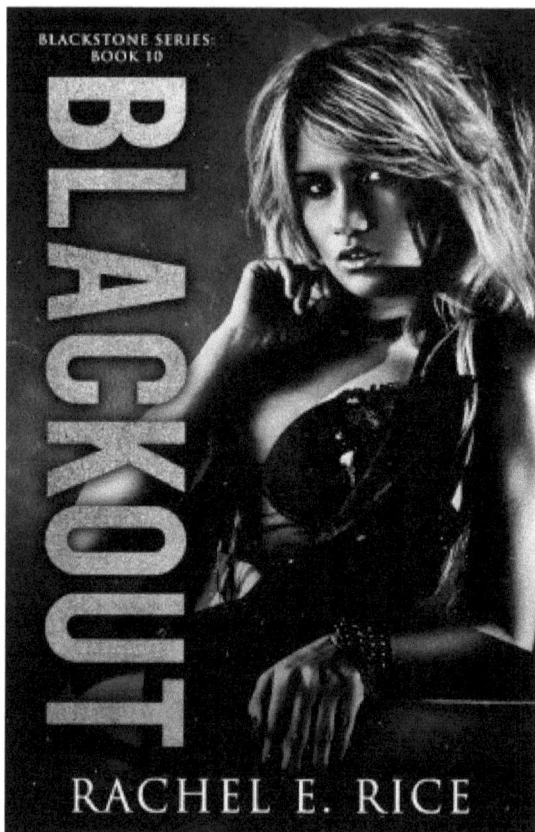

# Don't miss out!

Visit the website below and you can sign up to receive emails whenever Rachel E. Rice publishes a new book. There's no charge and no obligation.

https://books2read.com/r/B-A-QKZIC-LPAXE

**BOOKS 2 READ**

Connecting independent readers to independent writers.

# Also by Rachel E. Rice

**Blackstone, Book 1**
The Incredible Mr. Black
Temptation In Black
Submission To Black
Black Tie Affair
Mourning Becomes Black (Book 5)
The Incredible Mr. Black Box Set


**Captain and Virgin, Book1**
The Captain and The Virgin
The Captain's Lady and the Pirate
The Captain's Revenge: a Triangle of Love and Sex


**Insatiable**
Insatiable: The Lone Werewolf finds his Mate
Insatiable: A Werewolf's Hunger Book 2
Insatiable: A Werewolf's Wedding Book 3
Insatiable: The Werewolves' Challenge Book 4
Insatiable: Hunter's Moon Book 5
Insatiable: Moon Tide Book 6

Moon Rapture Book 7
Tracker Book 8
Thorn in Moonscape #9


**Obsession, Book1**
Obsession: Warm Bodies, Cold Hearts
Naked Obsession
Burning Obsession


**Seduction, Book 1**
Seduced by an Earl
The Naked Countess


**Standalone**
Finding Summer
One Desire
Insatiable Box Set
Insatiable Box Set: Books 1-4
Fade To Black Book 6
Insatiable: Damon in Moonscape #10
Moonscape Box Set
The Soul of A Vampire #1
The Soul of A Vampire Book 2
A Bride For A Werewolf: The Beginning
The Soul of A Vampire #3
The Soul of A Vampire Box Set
A Werewolf's Passion #11
I Am First Night Book 2 Night Series

I Am Last Night Book 3 Night Series
I Am The Night
To kill a Vampire
To Kill a Vampire Book 2
To Kill A Vampire Book 3
Back to Black (A Blackstone Novel)

Watch for more at www.rachel-e-rice.com.

# About the Author

My name is Rachel E. Rice. I have been writing since I was a teen. I enjoy reading and writing romance fiction.You can contact me at: rachelerice04@gmail.com; I have written several novels and short stories. My short reads are: The Captain and the Virgin; The Captain's Lady and the Pirate; The Captain's Revenge: a Triangle of Love and Sex; and two novellas: Book 1 Seduced by an Earl and Book 2: The Naked Countess. A historical novella set in 1960: Tamika Jade: The case of the Girl with the Rose Tattoo.My contemporary novels are: The Obsession series, which begins with Book 1: Warm Bodies, Cold Hearts; Book 2 in the series is Naked Obsession. Book 3 : Burning Obsession.These following books are erotic romances. Book 1: The Incredible Mr. Black. Book 2: Temptation in Black, and Book 3: Submission To Black. All books are available and books 4 Black Tie Affair and 5 Mourning Becomes Black was published in 2016. Coming soon Book 6, Fade To Black will be available in Jan. 2017.Because I enjoy writing in different genres, my New Adult novel: Finding Summer, is available for purchase as well as another stand-alone edition: One Desire.My Werewolf Series Book 1: Insatiable: The Lone Werewolf finds a Mate, and Book 2: Insatiable: A Werewolf's Hunger is available where all e-books are sold. Book 3 of the Insatiable Series is available as well as seven more books in this series.When I'm not writing, I am watching movies and riding throughout the U.S meeting people.I have a degree in education and I reside in Texas.

Read more at www.rachel-e-rice.com.

9 798227 866714